CHERRY AMES, DEPARTMENT STORE NURSE

The CHERRY AMES *Stories*

☆   ☆   ☆

The VICKI BARR *Flight Stewardess Series*

CHERRY AMES
DEPARTMENT
STORE NURSE

By

HELEN WELLS

~~~~~~

NEW YORK

GROSSET & DUNLAP

Publishers

8-10-63-238- Amer Pub Co

© BY GROSSET & DUNLAP, INC., 1956

Contents

Contents

CHERRY AMES,
DEPARTMENT STORE NURSE

~~~~~~

CHAPTER I

Home for Thanksgiving

"THIS," SAID CHERRY, "IS PRETTY WONDERFUL!" SHE beamed at the others around the festive table with its autumn fruits and flowers. Her family beamed back at her. "For once all four Ameses are together, and *isn't* it nice?"

"I feel a little selfish, not asking some of the relatives for Thanksgiving dinner," Mrs. Ames remarked.

"Just us is fine," said Charlie. "Besides, that leaves us more turkey."

Mr. Ames, who could carve only when standing up, muttered that it was about time Charlie took over this chore. But when Charlie obligingly stood up to help, their father said, "Never mind, thanks. No chores for either of you kids when you're only home for the holiday."

"I won't make any speeches about what it's worth to me to be here today," Cherry said. "Even for a few days' leave."

She had flown to Hilton, Illinois, from New York and this evening she would have to fly back again. If her old friend Ann Evans hadn't had family matters to tend to, she might be able to stay at home longer. On the other hand, if Ann Evans Powell hadn't needed someone in a hurry to substitute for her, Cherry would never have secured the nursing job in a New York department store, two weeks ago. And it *was* a fascinating job.

Conversation lapsed for a few minutes as the Ames family concentrated on Edith Ames's Thanksgiving feast.

"Best bird we ever had," said Mr. Ames happily.

"Especially considering that I popped him into the oven and went off to church services with the rest of you." Mrs. Ames added, "Cherry helped me with the dinner, you know. Honey, when you get married, remember that the way to a man's heart is through his stomach."

"I don't see Cherry getting married in any hurry," Charlie said. "Not until she finds someone she likes better than nursing."

Cherry glanced up; she had been thinking how different her big, comfortable, leisurely home was from the high jinks at No. 9 Standish Street in Greenwich Village. She had merely intended to visit the Spencer Club girls for a few days; instead, she'd inherited Ann's job, and stayed on with her old classmates from Spencer Nursing School.

"All right, smarty," she said to her brother. "Since you're so knowing, I'll surprise you and tell you there *is* someone in my romance department."

"A handsome young doctor? Couldn't be anything else."

"Now don't tease Cherry about her nursing," their mother said gently. "Anyone who's been as devoted as she has—"

"Who's the lucky young man?" Mr. Ames demanded.

"Oh, Dad! It's nothing much, really. I mean not so soon." Cherry turned rosy to the roots of her dark curls. "Mostly I'm teasing Charlie. I understand he's interested in someone himself."

"Won't talk?" Charlie laughed. "Then neither will I."

"Who's ready for second helpings?" Mrs. Ames asked.

Cherry knew her mother's tactful maneuver of pretending to be uninterested, and knew perfectly well that the subject would come up again later. She was glad, though, to have a respite from her brother's teasing. When they had been small, growing up together, and then particularly in their teens, Charlie with his teasing had been the bane of her existence.

"Come on, Cherry," said her father, "tell us his name."

Cherry's dark eyes danced and she shook her head. "I'll tell you, though, about a pretty special person who really has me interested."

"Someone at Thomas and Parke's?"

"Yes, Mother. That department store is chock-full of interesting people. It's a whole world in itself. Well, her name is Mrs. Julian. Anna Elizabeth Julian, and from the few words we've exchanged, I think she's someone I'd like to know better."

Cherry's family peppered her with questions. She tried to answer everybody at once, and enjoy Thanksgiving turkey at the same time. No, she hardly knew Mrs. Julian—Cherry was so new on the job she didn't know many people yet—but liked the young woman's lovely, fragile appearance and friendly manner. Cherry had been struck by her extreme shyness, an unexpected trait in business. Mrs. Julian sold art objects and antiques. Fabulous things like porcelains and flowery Aubusson carpets and painted Venetian furniture and Chinese jade. Mrs. Julian apparently knew a great deal about art objects; only another woman and a man, besides the department head, were qualified to deal in these museum pieces.

"Emerald earrings that belonged to a queen, and

Mother, what a collection of fans!" Cherry exclaimed. "A real treasure house, that department. . . . Yes, Charlie, I *do* spend my time in the store's hospital. Working. Antiques are located on the same floor as the medical department, the sixth floor, along with the personnel office and the—"

Cherry broke off short. Charlie grinned.

"The what?"

"Oh, nothing."

"We will now," Mrs. Ames announced, "have our pumpkin pie and coffee. Charlie, dear, will you help clear the table?"

"You women certainly stick together," Charlie complained, but he kissed their mother lightly on the cheek. "If anyone took an equal interest in *my* job, I'd be complimented."

"We already know all about your job," Mr. Ames pointed out.

Charlie worked in Indianapolis, near home, in the engineering division of a large automotive plant. The only fault he could find with his job was that it did not involve airplanes—he had flown as an Air Force pilot—but at any rate he was working with machinery and speed.

In fact, he sprinted out with the platters so fast that his mother pleaded for the safety of her best china. Mr. Ames refused to help this once, and sat contentedly in the armchair at the head of the table.

"Faster, you slaves. Cherry, that's a mighty pretty red dress you're wearing. Matches your cheeks."

"Thank you, Dad. You always were partial to red."

"Well, I'm partial to my daughter. If there's a young man in New York you're interested in, I'd like to have a look at him."

"Why, Dad! I'm not that serious."

Her father grunted. "You never can tell what will happen."

During the balance of dinner, Cherry's mother kept the questions to what nursing in a New York department store was like. The two Ames men were foiled.

This Thanksgiving afternoon was gray and windy, not a promising day for a walk. The big house grew quiet. Charlie went across the street to see Bob Pritchett. Cherry's mother was resting now, for some neighbors had promised to come in later. Her father was in the living room reading a book. How quiet it was! For a few moments Cherry stood listening to the tick of the grandfather clock on the stair landing. It hadn't been peaceful or quiet at the girls' boarding school where she recently had been nurse-in-charge, but it had been a lot of fun! This new department store assignment was fun, too, though it certainly was never very quiet in New York!

"Well, if I enjoy the peace and quiet at home so much," Cherry challenged herself, "why don't I stay home? There ought to be two of me, one to go gal-livanting around nursing, and one to stay home and love it."

She did care deeply for this house, and for this small town. Her grandparents, and their parents, had lived here. As she went up the long staircase Cherry touched the polished stair rail, which had heel nicks where she and Charlie used to slide down. In her own gay red-and-white room she gazed out at the garden and yard below. The lilac bush brushed her windows with bare branches, and her mother's flower beds looked straggly. Perhaps she was lucky, with winter setting in, to be returning to a great city with all its activity and brilliance. And new people to get better acquainted with, like Tom Reese and Mrs. Julian.

Cherry was halfway through her packing when her mother peeked in.

"What are you smiling to yourself about?"

"Come in, Mother." Cherry pulled the door open and offered her mother the small slipper chair.

"I hate to see you packing. This visit has been so short."

"Awfully good, though," Cherry said. "We've talked constantly for two days and two evenings now. We had so much news to catch up on."

"Yet in all our talking you didn't mention any romance."

Cherry laughed and ran her hand through her dark curls in a gesture of despair.

"All right, all right! His name is Tom Reese, he's assistant to the store manager, and besides that, he supervises the sixth and seventh floors. He sort of floats around the store wherever he's needed. But his office is right next door to the medical department."

Cherry's mother smiled. "Is he very nice?"

"As far as I know, yes. I know him only in the store. Everybody there likes him. Tom Reese has been very nice and helpful to me, helping me step overnight into Ann's job."

"Well, it all sounds pleasant," said Mrs. Ames. "I suppose you and he and everyone at Thomas and Parke's will be extremely busy with the Christmas rush?"

"You're so right. I hadn't thought of that."

The ringing of the doorbell interrupted their conversation.

"The Pritchetts!" Cherry's mother exclaimed. "And I haven't even washed my face! Cherry, go downstairs and help Dad entertain them."

Cherry always enjoyed seeing their old neighbors again. Presently the Galloways came in to join the Ames family on Thanksgiving afternoon. But the ones Cherry most wanted to see—Dr. Joseph Fortune and his daughter, Midge—had driven up to Chicago for today. However, news of them was good: Dr. Joe seemed happy in administering the Hilton Clinic, and Midge was struggling through high school in her usual harum-scarum way. So Cherry felt satisfied about the Fortunes.

Old friends might be the best, but as dusk came, Cherry wished the visitors would not stay much longer. She had only an hour left before plane time. Finally, their neighbors understandingly left.

Then, with the living room cleared, and only the four Ameses occupying it, no one could think of much to say.

"Hope you have a good flight, Cherry."

"I think I will, Charlie."

A pause. Mr. Ames contributed: "The weather prediction is clear."

"They're not always right, though," said Cherry's mother. "Still, I see a star is out."

The hands of the clock went around so slowly that Cherry realized, half-ashamed, how much she longed to be on her way. To be up to her ears in nursing and people! She said good-by lightheartedly to her family.

"Good-by, honey, and good luck—your new job sounds intriguing," Cherry's mother said. "But promise me you'll be home for Christmas! You, too, Charles."

They promised to try their best. Cherry quickly kissed her father and mother *au revoir*. Then Charlie drove her to Hilton Airport.

CHAPTER II

New Friends, Old Friends

CHERRY WOKE UP FRIDAY MORNING WITH A SLIGHT sense of dislocation. This must be No. 9, because hunched in the other twin bed she could see Gwen's familiar red hair and a curve of freckled cheek. Cherry had let herself in sleepily after midnight and found the apartment dark, all her fellow nurses asleep.

"I'll bet nobody even knows I'm here this morning," Cherry thought. She sat up and rubbed her eyes. In that case she could beat the others into the one bathroom and squeeze in a shower.

"Good morning, Cherry," Gwen yawned. "I see you're back again." She leaned over and whacked Cherry on the back. "Ha-ha! *Your* back again! Get it?"

Cherry groaned. "Please, not so early in the morning. How's your aunt? Did she stuff you with turkey?"

"We gobbled the gobbler!" When Cherry said *ouch*, Gwen struggled to a sitting position. "Don't blame me. It's that punny Betty Lane. I caught pun-itis from her."

Betty Lane was staying at No. 9 temporarily. She, too, had earned her R.N. at Spencer, but a year after Cherry and her friends had graduated. Therefore, Betty was only an honorary member of that august body, the Spencer Club. She was a pleasant girl, except for one thing, Cherry discovered—Betty had just beat her to the shower.

Cherry took one look at her wrist watch—she'd forgotten to turn it ahead an hour, upon returning east. Golly! No time for breakfast. She'd better hustle! Cherry washed in haste, practically jumped into her clothes, and called:

"Gwen? Ready to walk to the subway with me?"

"Gwen just left," Vivian called from one of the other small bedrooms. "That's what she gets for working way out on Long Island. Bertha said to tell you hello and good-by."

"Mai Lee? . . . Oh, she's visiting friends, isn't she?" Cherry pulled on her coat. " 'By, kids. See you at dinner."

The remaining two, rushing for their own jobs, called mumbled good-bys to her. "Well," Cherry thought, "I just hope the people at the department store aren't *all* in this scrambled state."

Cherry checked in at Thomas and Parke's a little earlier than the crowd of employees. She walked quickly across the main floor toward the bank of elevators. What a surprise! Yesterday while the store was closed, the display artists had transformed the main floor into a Christmas festival. Giant artificial snow-flakes sparkled and spun slowly overhead, while fantastic cherubim hovered high over the counters. The counters themselves were heaped with bright, plentiful new stock for the Christmas season, and there would be music as soon as the doors opened for business.

They were rushing the season, it seemed to Cherry, but all the stores now followed this calendar of merchandising. She felt a little relieved, all the same, to step out of the elevator on the sixth floor and find that it was still November here, without any trace of decorations.

Of course there was decoration and beauty enough in the glass cases and fine furniture of the antiques department, where the night watchman was making the last of his rounds. The big personnel department, at the far end of this floor, was already bustling with activity, hiring new employees for the seasonal rush.

"Good morning, Miss Ames, good morning," her assistant sang out as Cherry entered the medical department. "How are we this morning?"

"Oh, just fine, I guess, Gladys. How are you?"

Gladys Green was a brand-new, young R.N., bouncing with enthusiasm. This was her first job and Cherry wished Gladys were a shade less determined to do good. She had, Cherry saw, rearranged the first-aid cabinet, the nursing instruments, and even, in the small partitioned room beyond, moved the two cots.

"Better, isn't it?" Gladys said cheerfully.

"It's very nice, though you'll have to show me where you've put things."

The infirmary, like most store infirmaries, was small and compact enough for her to be able to find things. Only small emergencies were treated here; anyone seriously ill would be treated by Dr. Murphy, whose office was around the corner. Absences due to illness were checked by the personnel department working together with the State Bureau of Compensation. Nursing here, Cherry reflected as she changed into white uniform and cap and white shoes, did not call on the more difficult nursing skills, like surgery or obstetrics, but it did place her on her own in full charge. Sound judgment about people and rapid, right decisions about health were the main requirements.

Gladys Green rose respectfully, to permit Cherry to occupy the one desk.

"Thanks, Gladys. Did you have any emergencies during the few days I was away?"

"Honestly, it was so quiet I didn't know what to do with myself! To tell you the truth, that's *half* the reason why I moved the equipment around."

Cherry grinned. "May I see the daily report sheets?"

Gladys gave them to her, then stood reading them solemnly over Cherry's shoulder.

"You did very well," Cherry said, reading: a cut finger; a sprained ankle; a head cold; a few other small emergencies. Then there was a woman customer who fell on the escalator, and a man in the shipping room who received a deep cut from broken glass. Nurse Green had administered first aid and sent them, with a store escort, to Dr. Murphy.

"I'll bet you I could have treated them perfectly well myself," the young nurse said.

"I'll bet you couldn't. I'll bet *I* couldn't. Any nurse who tries to play doctor isn't a very responsible nurse, you know."

"That's just what Ann Powell told me."

"Cheer up, Gladys, we won't have many slow periods now that Christmas shopping is starting."

"You're right. Listen." The hum of many people walking and talking, the metallic click of elevator doors, telephones ringing, indicated that the store was open now to customers.

This was a good chance, Cherry said, for them to check on supplies, and put the medical department in shipshape order. And Cherry took care to praise her assistant, who was trying so hard to do a good job.

The two nurses had been working for about an hour when someone knocked on the open door. It was Tom Reese, holding by the hand a small, tear-smudged boy.

"Good morning, Miss Ames. How would you like to take care of a young fellow who got separated from his mother?"

Cherry smiled at Tom Reese who looked startlingly like her, vividly dark, lively, quick-moving—like more of a twin than Charlie. Then Cherry smiled at the youngster and held out her hand.

"I was just wishing for a boy to help me count boxes. What's your name?"

"Bobby. I want my mamma."

"Your mamma will be here in a few minutes. How high can you count, Bobby?"

The small boy stopped to think. "Twenty-five. Have you got more'n twenty-five boxes?"

"Well, we'd better go see. First, Miss Green, let's help Bobby off with his heavy coat, and give him a drink of water."

Gladys took charge of Bobby for the moment, and Cherry turned to Tom Reese. He explained that the child's mother would quickly be located via the store's loud-speaker system. Then he said:

"I can count to a million or so, if you'll need another helper. Did you have a good trip home?"

"Awfully good, thank you."

Tom Reese's dark eyes sparkled with friendliness.
"Brace yourself for the big rush. If you need me, remember my office is right next door."

As he left, Gladys looked up from washing
Bobby's face, a knowing grin on her face. Cherry
pretended to pay no attention, and Bobby declared,
"That man's nice!"

Bobby's mother arrived soon afterward, and then
a small stream of minor casualties kept Cherry and her
assistant occupied. A man from the upholstery department came in holding a handkerchief over one
eye. Cherry carefully, deftly, removed the lint particle which could cause surprising pain. Then she
applied a soothing hot compress. "Don't rub your
eyes," she cautioned the patient, "and don't use eye
cups. Their pressure is harmful, and they can carry
infection. If your eye feels sensitive, come back and
I'll bathe it with a weak boric acid solution—using
a sterilized eye dropper." The man thanked her and
said he'd learned something.

A brief lull was interrupted by a saleswoman who
complained of a sore throat. Cherry checked the
woman over and said, "That 'sore throat' looks to me
like strep throat, Mrs. Crane." Strep was infectious
and everyone in this woman's department might catch

it. "I'd like you to visit Dr. Murphy at once, Mrs.
Crane. I'll phone him, and Miss Green will make
out a medical pass for you to give your supervisor—"

So it went, all day Friday. Nothing crucial, but
every case was important.

The next day there was no free time. Cherry and
Gladys Green treated an assortment of customers and
employees for minor ailments. Tom Reese poked his
head in the door around noon to say:

"The main floor is beginning to look like a foot-
ball scrimmage. Busy in here?"

"Well, I'd say we're earning our salaries." Cherry
smiled back at him. "But I'm glad to be on a compar-
atively quiet floor. Antiques, apparently, are too costly
to attract crowds."

"You should see the toy department. That reminds
me! I'll have some toys sent here, because you two
gals are going to have *lots* more mislaid children."

"Thank you, Mr. Reese."

"Everybody calls me Tom." He waved and was
gone.

By Saturday evening Cherry was glad enough to
go home to No. 9 and just sit down in the one comfortable armchair.

Only Bertha and Gwen were there, the others
having gone out to a favorite restaurant around the
corner. Bertha, who was No. 9's best and therefore
chief cook, seemed rather hurt.

"Never mind," said Cherry to the big, handsome girl who still retained the wholesome outdoor look of a farm girl. "The three of us will rustle up something better than they can buy."

Gwen kicked off her shoes and flopped down on the sofa. "Jeepers, what a day! I like lab work, all except the standing up part. No, you *know* I can't work properly perched on a stool. Dr. Hall still doesn't believe that!"

They chatted a bit about their respective jobs. Bertha was in charge of a children's hospital ward and loved it. Privately they agreed they would not enjoy Betty Lane's job as nurse-companion to a well-to-do elderly woman. They'd rather do real nursing. Somehow talking together quickened their professional pride and erased the day's trivial annoyances. Cherry turned on the radio for music, and Gwen, with a grandiloquent air, passed a tray of tomato-juice cocktails. Presently Bertha rustled up supper. They were having such a comfortable time as a threesome that it startled them when the telephone rang.

Gwen's aunt was calling from Long Island, with an interesting offer. Gwen relayed it to Cherry and Bertha. . . . "Yes, I'm listening to you, Aunt Kathy. . . . Hey, kids, she wants me and one of you Spencer Clubbers to stay with her for a while!"

"Where?" Cherry murmured. She felt an interest, since she and Gwen were old tried-and-true roommates.

"Long Island. . . . Where is Uncle John going on Sunday? . . . Arabia? Good heavens!"

Bertha muttered something about Gwen's uncle being in the oil business. Gwen's face changed expression so rapidly that the other two could not figure out the rest of the conversation. Gwen hung up.

"Aunt Kathy is a love. She says she wants young company in that big house, and whichever two of us—"

A scrambling at the door interrupted them. The door suddenly swung open and Vivian, Mai Lee, and Betty Lane all but fell in. "I told you someone would forget to lock it again!" Vivian insisted, picking up her hat from the floor. Cherry had to smile at the sight of them. Mai Lee was tiny, like an ivory figurine; Vivian was a pretty girl of middle height; while Betty Lane rose to six feet, managing to look stately and dignified—which she wasn't.

"Good morning, welcome home, and good evening, Cherry," said Mai Lee and composedly sat down.

Betty Lane inquired if everybody's Thanksgiving had been as happy as hers.

"Terrific, except that's ancient history by now." Gwen moved over and made room on the sofa. The young women commenced to chatter.

"Has anyone seen Ann Evans this week? Are she and her husband back from Boston yet?"

"Who's the stunning young man who drives you home from work, Betty? You never told us you have a beau."

"Whoever took my thermometer by mistake," Vivian said plaintively, "please give it back by to-morrow. Somebody here has two."

Gwen raised her voice to announce that her aunt had room for an extra, unspecified Spencer Clubber and in the interests of democratic procedure she, Gwen, was giving one and all present a chance to accept. No one heard her, except Cherry.

"Shall I make my announcement all over again?"

"No, please don't—because I'd like to live out on Long Island with you," Cherry said. "I love being cramped in No. 9, but—"

"I was hoping for that." Gwen's crinkled-up eyes seemed to dance. "Commuting, I warn you. Though you're welcome to use my car out there. Now, how soon can you get a day off to move out there?"

"I'll find out. What day is good for you?"

Gwen and Cherry compared dates. Bertha and Betty argued about the merits of a new prosthetic device, while Mai Lee and Vivian shared the telephone in a visit with Ann.

"The Spencer Club," said Cherry to Gwen, "won't realize two of its tenants are going until we've

actually gone. Try again to tell them, why don't you?
And you know—I'm just delighted."

After a good rest on Sunday, Cherry reported for
work bright and early Monday morning. Her eager
young assistant was in first again. "I suspect you sleep
here." Cherry smiled at Gladys Green, who had already dusted and straightened up the medical department.

It was a good thing Gladys had made everything
ready, because on Monday mornings, as a rule, people seemed to be accident and ailment prone—and
this Monday was no exception. A regular procession
of sneezes, splinters, bad scratches, upset stomachs,
and headaches went on all morning. Even Tom
Reese's secretary, the calm-as-a-lake Miss Josephson,
came in for an aspirin. Cherry was more out of breath
than alarmed. At half past twelve the medical department quieted down and Cherry tried to catch up on
her paper work. She sent Gladys out for lunch hour,
asking her to bring back a sandwich and milk. Gladys
offered to remain.

"You stayed in while I was in Hilton, so now it's
my turn," Cherry said.

Later it seemed to Cherry as if some sixth sense
had warned her that she would be needed.

She was busy making out reports when she happened to turn and look out into the wide corridor.

Mrs. Julian, supported by the small elderly woman who worked with her in the antiques department, was walking slowly, uncertainly toward the medical department.

Cherry hurried out and helped Mrs. Julian to a cot. She was crying a little and seemed dazed. She kept saying in a low, hysterical voice:

"But I don't know, I simply don't know! Please believe me, of course I didn't! Please—please—"

"What happened?" Cherry whispered to the elderly woman.

"She started to faint, right there on the sales floor, then she started babbling—"

"I see. Lie down, Mrs. Julian, please try to relax. Don't talk." Cherry helped her to a supine position and drew a light blanket over her. The woman was tense and trembling. Cherry chafed her wrists and removed her shoes.

"Why did she faint? Has she been ill, Mrs.—"

"I'm Miss Lamb, Janet Lamb. No, she hasn't been ill that I know of. Mrs. Julian has had a distressing morning. Such a shock and ordeal for her—"

"Bad news? Family troubles?" Cherry checked the woman's pulse and breathing; this was not a heart attack, thank heavens.

"No, Nurse, not family. I don't think she has any family left. A bad experience here in the store. Will she be all right?"

"*Lie down, Mrs. Julian. Please try to relax.*"

Cherry hesitated. "Well, we'll let her rest for fifteen minutes, and then if she isn't quieter, I'll call a doctor."

Poor Miss Lamb looked pale and upset herself. Cherry advised her not to worry.

"If there's anything more you can do, I'll call you, Miss Lamb."

"Thank you. I— It's so unlike Mrs. Julian to lose her self-control. She's such a reserved young woman. Well, then, I'll go back and tell Mr. Dance and Adam Heller that she probably will be quite all right soon."

Cherry watched her patient carefully for the next five minutes. She did not believe the reassuring fib she had told Miss Lamb. The patient was young, but she was a person of frail constitution and high-strung nerves, judging by the slight frame under the blanket and the finely drawn face. A person of this sort could be made gravely ill by shock.

"Please—please—I don't know," the woman repeated. "I can't imagine where it went to—"

"Mrs. Julian," Cherry said, gentle but firm, "listen to me. You are here to rest."

The blue eyes fluttered and focused on Cherry's face. "A nurse? Where am I?"

"In the medical department. You fainted. But you're going to be all right, and you must rest now."

The young woman sighed. "I feel so tired."

"Try to sleep, Mrs. Julian."

"Will you tell them—?"

"Yes. There's nothing to worry about. Just sleep."
Cherry did not know what her patient was trying to
convey, but for the moment that did not matter.

Presently the blue eyes, as bewildered and trusting
as a child's, closed. Mrs. Julian's hands uncurled and
her breathing grew slower, deeper. Cherry covered
her with another blanket. She signaled to Gladys,
who had just returned, to close the door. If she could
persuade Mrs. Julian to talk, it had better be in private.

CHAPTER III

The Jade Vase

THE EXHAUSTED WOMAN HAD BEEN SLEEPING for half an hour now. Cherry, watching her, felt satisfied that a doctor's services were not necessary.

"She looks as if she has always been protected," Cherry thought, smoothing back the young woman's fair, fine hair from her forehead. Even in sleep, the forehead was creased with a frown. "Wish I knew more about her, then I'd be better equipped to help her."

Cherry had an idea. She scribbled a note of inquiry, and moving quietly to the door, asked her assistant to deliver it to Tom Reese next door, or if he was out, to his secretary. "Hurry, please." Tom Reese made it part of his job to know personally dozens of the store staff; an answer from him ought to be more revealing than a cut-and-dried report from the personnel department.

A few minutes later Tom Reese himself softly opened the door.

"Sorry, Mr. Reese, but—" Cherry shook her head, motioning him to stay out.

He beckoned her to the other side of the door for a moment. Luckily, no other patient was in the medical department. Gladys slipped in to watch Mrs. Julian. Tom Reese's dark eyes questioned hers.

"You know there was a theft, don't you? A valuable Ming vase. It's valued at about a thousand dollars."

"So that's it! But how is a gentle person like Mrs. Julian involved?"

"Haven't time now to tell you the details. I'm expecting an important phone call. What is it you need to know about her?"

"Something about her background. What sort of person she is—"

Tom Reese rapidly told Cherry these facts: Anna Elizabeth Julian, who was about thirty, came from a respected and cultivated family. As a girl she had traveled widely in Europe with her family; they had collected art treasures and antiques, and Anna Elizabeth became something of an expert. Later, she had married happily, but her happiness had been cut short by a series of illnesses and deaths. First she had lost her parents, then her husband. Tom Reese did not know the details. He did know that the family fi-

nances and estate had been managed so extravagantly
that almost nothing was left for Mrs. Julian. Without
business training or experience, she cast about for a
way to earn her living. Selling antiques at Thomas
and Parke's, "or rather, for Mr. Dance," Tom Reese
corrected himself, was her first job.

"She needs her job, Miss Cherry. That's everything I know. Hope it helps you. Now I have to run."

"Thanks very much. You always make store matters so clear to me, Mr. Reese."

"Tom," he insisted, smiled, and left.

The young woman was still asleep, a light and
fretful doze. Cherry sat down beside her to wait. She
thought over the brief life history which the young
store executive had outlined. What extremes this
fair-haired Anna Elizabeth had experienced! Well,
she must really know antiques or the store would not
employ her. Wait, Tom Reese had said, "She sells
for Mr. Dance." For a second Cherry was puzzled,
than recalled an explanation Tom Reese had made
on her first day when she was trying to get acquainted
with the sixth floor.

The antiques and art objects department, the young
executive had said, like some other departments, was
not owned and operated by the store. Antiques was
a concession, that is, a separate business belonging to
Willard Dance. Mr. Dance, the concessionaire, paid
the store a percentage of his profits, guaranteeing to

pay a certain minimum sum. In exchange he received floor space within the store, use of the Thomas and Parke name, and store services. Services? That meant, Cherry reasoned, that the store was obligated to provide protection for the art objects; for instance, night watchmen and store detectives.

Her patient stirred, sighed, and seemed about to wake. Cherry felt Mrs. Julian's pulse again; it was stronger now. The woman drifted back to sleep. Poor thing, she must have had an exhausting time of it. Perhaps her department head, Mr. Dance, would come in.

Cherry had seen but not yet met him. He must be a wealthy man, she thought, to operate an art department with its valuable treasures, and he must be a connoisseur as well. No, not necessarily wealthy, because like many art and antique dealers, Tom Reese had explained, Mr. Dance obtained merchandise on a consignment basis. That is, when an individual or estate had paintings, fine antique furniture, rare rugs, or other valuables it wished to dispose of, it sent these things on consignment (almost a loan) to Mr. Dance. He attempted to sell them, and when successful, kept a percentage of the sale price as his fee. It all had sounded to Cherry so much more colorful than other businesses, and probably no more of a gamble.

"Nurse?"

"Yes, I'm here, Mrs. Julian."

"Heavens, I must have slept a long time!" Mrs. Julian sat up, rather embarrassed.

"Not quite an hour. You look refreshed and like yourself again."

A little pink showed in her cheeks, which were still tear-streaked. Cherry offered a wash basin and asked whether Mrs. Julian didn't feel a little thirsty or hungry. But Mrs. Julian was self-consciously getting off the cot, smoothing her black silk dress.

"What *must* you all think of me! How can I ever go out there and face people after having made such a spectacle of myself?" She made a half-humorous face but her nervousness was noticeable.

Cherry gently made her sit down again. "For one thing, you are not going anywhere until I've given you at least a cup of hot tea, and filled out a medical fact sheet for you. For another thing, Mrs. Julian, anyone can show the effects of strain. Don't blame yourself."

Mrs. Julian accepted a cup of tea. Presently, shyly, she said, "I'll be *glad* to talk to someone I can trust. Nurses are bound by the same Hippocratic oath as doctors, or something similar, aren't they?"

"Yes, indeed we are."

Reassured, Mrs. Julian said anxiously that she did not want to do anything which might offend her employer, Mr. Dance.

"He's been so kind to me, Miss Ames. How many businessmen would have given me a chance at a job, inexperienced as I am?"

Mrs. Julian explained that Mr. Dance knew of her and her late family's interest in collecting rare, beautiful things; his late wife had pursued the same interest. He had suggested to Mrs. Julian that she might like to work in his department. It was a boon to her, an unexpected piece of good fortune. Mr. Dance had requested the store's personnel department to interview her and hire her. She supposed now that either the personnel department or Mr. Dance could fire her.

"But why would anyone want to fire you, Mrs. Julian?"

"I don't think Willard Dance wants to, but the personnel department may—" The woman twisted her handkerchief into a hard ball. "After this morning—"

Painfully, with self-control, Mrs. Julian reconstructed for Cherry the extraordinary events of that morning.

One of her department's treasures was a small, rare, jade Ming vase. Small enough to fit into an overcoat pocket or a handbag. It was one of a group of jade pieces kept under lock and key in a glass display cabinet. Only Mr. Dance and Mrs. Julian had keys to the cabinet holding the jade. Not that Mr. Dance didn't place full confidence in Miss Janet Lamb and old Adam Heller, Mrs. Julian hastened to explain—"but they're so absent-minded about things like keys."

Mrs. Julian said, "I showed the tiny vase this morning to a customer. He seemed really eager to buy it. Naturally he asked to see several other jade things, too, as a basis for comparison, though they weren't nearly so valuable. So there I was, showing this man the vase and five other pieces which I can name exactly, when—when it disappeared."

"Disappeared! But how could it?" Cherry asked.

"That's just it, Miss Ames—I don't know! I walked away from the vase there on the table for just a few seconds—but the customer followed me."

"Who else was in the department at the time?"

"Quite a few people."

Mrs. Julian said that generally only two or three people and a few store messengers would be browsing and passing through the antiques department. Today many more people than usual came to admire their collection because of a special sale advertisement. "I remember noticing Miss Lamb and Mr. Heller at the far end of the sales floor from me, busy with customers of their own. And Mr. Dance, who has the one other key to the jade cabinet, was out of the store to visit a gallery that's closing out."

"With a crowd," Cherry said, "there might have been a shoplifter."

"The store detectives don't think so," Mrs. Julian said stiffly, and resumed. "Mr. Dance returned while we were searching for the vase. He and the store detectives, whom he immediately summoned, considered the customer not guilty. For one reason, the customer wanted to *buy* the vase, and was very much distressed at its disappearance."

"Was he a customer you knew, or a stranger?" Cherry asked.

"I'd never seen the man until today, but the store knows him—he's an old charge customer."

The man had willingly submitted to an examination of his garments by store detectives. They had not found the vase on him. He willingly agreed to submit to further investigation by insurance company detectives. Every treasure in the department was insured by its owner; Mr. Dance insisted on this. The store in its turn insisted that Mr. Dance carry insurance, too, on the art objects in his keeping.

"It looks to me," Cherry said thoughtfully, "as if a shoplifter took the vase."

"Or as if *I* took it," Mrs. Julian stated sadly. "Yes, Miss Ames, at least some of the detectives suspect me. I was the last person known to handle the Ming vase."

Cherry couldn't believe anyone would be suspicious of a woman who seemed so gentle and transparently honest as Anna Elizabeth Julian. Her bearing, everything about her, proclaimed her an honorable and sensitive person.

"Has any shoplifter," Cherry asked, "been caught in any other part of the store today?"

"Not that Mr. Dance or I know of. Unluckily, suspicion has fallen on me. Mr. Dance is as distressed as I am. He's being wonderful about the whole thing and doing his best to clear me. Just the same—"

Mrs. Julian told Cherry that she, too, as well as the customer had been searched and questioned. Executives from relevant departments—jewelry and silver—were at once alerted of the theft. Store detectives and New York City detectives were informed at once, and also the insurance company detectives, that the Ming vase was missing. For two hours in a private "protection" office on the seventh floor, an inquiry was carried on. It was a grueling experience for Mrs. Julian. When she was permitted to return to the sales floor, she fainted.

"No wonder," said Cherry. "Still, as long as Mr. Dance stands ready to vouch for you, you shouldn't worry too much."

Mrs. Julian couldn't help herself, she began to cry.

"Maybe it will turn out that the little vase has been mislaid," Cherry said.

"No, it has not been mislaid," Mrs. Julian got out. "We've already searched thoroughly."

Cherry knew of nothing to do or say, to comfort her, except let her talk of what troubled her.

"Mr. Dance has hinted to me, as gently and kindly as he could, that he might not be able to protect me against the store detectives who suspect me, and against the criticism of some executives. I—I may lose my job or be arrested."

"Surely not," Cherry murmured. She was shocked.

"Or I may have to pay back the value of the Ming vase." Mrs. Julian buried her face in her hands. "How can I? I have nothing. Nothing. And I swear I didn't take the vase!"

But just as quickly as she had broken down, Anna Elizabeth Julian gained control of herself. She sat erect, and wiped her eyes.

"I'm going back to the sales floor now," she announced.

"Don't you think it would be better to go home on a sick pass, instead of trying to work the rest of the day?" Cherry showed her the pass she had written out.

"No, thank you anyway, Miss Ames. I must remain here the rest of the afternoon. It's perhaps one small way of showing people that I'm innocent."

"Good for you, Mrs. Julian." Cherry gave her instructions on how to take care of herself after today's ordeal, and asked her to keep in touch.

"I will. It's been a help to talk. I— It sounds odd, but I feel you're a friend as well a nurse."

"That's part of being a good nurse."

For the rest of that troubled Monday, Cherry did her job adequately but with half of her mind on the Ming vase puzzle. She felt convinced that the direct-spoken, trusting woman had told the exact truth about the jade vase.

Before leaving the store at the end of the day, Cherry stepped next door and asked the secretary whether Mr. Reese was free to see her for a few minutes. She had to wait a bit, watching several people come and go through the store manager's office. Then Tom Reese came out to the reception room, looking tired and harassed.

He sat down beside Cherry on the leather couch. "See that wiry little man just going out? That's Hal Pierce, one of the store detectives. He's convinced Mrs. Julian pocketed the vase this morning, and slipped it to a confederate who then walked out of the store with it."

"Has Pierce any basis for such a claim?" Cherry asked. "Besides, how *could* she have pocketed it right under her customer's nose?"

"Pierce says the hand is quicker than the eye. She could have distracted him. Sorry if I don't state

Pierce's case very clearly. I'm tired; it's been a rough day. No fun grilling people, I can tell you, especially a nice person like Mrs. Julian. Is she feeling better?"

Cherry nodded, and told Tom Reese some of what Mrs. Julian had said concerning her innocence.

"Do you think she's guilty, Tom?"

"I'm not able to say much at this point, except that she is definitely under suspicion," he said. "Speaking purely personally, my impression of her is that she's a person of good faith. I think so, because Dance has only good things to say of her, and because, when Thomas and Parke first hired her, a bonding company investigated and bonded her. That speaks well for her."

"In that case—"

"But let's be hardheaded, Miss Cherry. This is a business concern and we can't be guided by our sympathies alone. We don't know Mrs. Julian well enough, either you or I, to be able to swear that she wouldn't take the vase."

Cherry supposed he was right to speak and think guardedly. All the same, she'd like to help Mrs. Julian clear herself, if she could. Cherry said so, as she stood up to go, and Tom Reese replied:

"Don't you suppose several of us feel the same way? Thanks for coming in. Let me know if I can help."

Next, Cherry stopped at the antiques department.

Mrs. Julian, looking extremely tired, was standing before a collection of old clocks and totaling her sales checks for the day. She smiled when she saw the white-clad nurse.

"You came to check up on me."

"I certainly did."

"I'm all right. It's good of you to take an interest."

"I also came," Cherry said, "to ask if you'd have lunch with me tomorrow."

"I'd love it! Can we get out of this wretched store? Say, the Mary White Restaurant. Let's plan to lunch together at noon tomorrow, then."

~~~~~~

CHAPTER IV

An Invitation

NEXT MORNING, CHERRY FOUND A MESSAGE WAITING
for her. Mr. Willard Dance wished to see Miss
Ames, at her convenience. Cherry was rather surprised, and curious to meet him. She completed the
usual first-thing-in-the-morning reports, mail, and
chores. Then she walked across the corridor to the
antiques display.

She knew Mr. Dance by sight, a tall, thin, big-
shouldered man with an unusually pleasant face. He
had a pleasant voice and manner, too.

"Hello, Miss Ames! I hope I haven't cut into your
morning's work too badly?"

"Not at all, Mr. Dance. I've been wanting to meet
you."

"Well, it's the gentleman's role to call on the lady,
even in business, I'd say. I would have come to you,

except that after the theft of a Ming vase here yesterday—" He drew his hand across his balding forehead.
"Of course you know about it, you treated Anna Julian, for which I'm very grateful."

Cherry glanced around for a glimpse of Mrs.
Julian's bright hair. She saw elderly Adam Heller
standing beside a suit of armor which dwarfed him,
showing two men how the visor worked. She saw
Miss Janet Lamb lovingly dusting a table display of
paperweights. But Mrs. Julian was nowhere in sight.

"She didn't come in today," Mr. Dance said, guessing Cherry's thoughts. "Mrs. Julian told me last
evening as she left the store that she believed she'd
rest today, and of course I was all for it. She had a
dreadful day yesterday, really harrowing."

Cherry murmured that she, too, was glad Mrs.
Julian was resting, but felt a little surprised that she
had not sent word she would not keep their lunch
date today. It did not seem like Mrs. Julian to be
rude. Was she being evasive?

Cherry was not sure what to think of Mr. Dance,
either. She half expected him to check up with her
on Mrs. Julian's health. However, he courteously
began showing her some of the lovely art objects
nearby.

"It's a great pleasure to deal in beautiful things,
Miss Ames, as you can imagine. Have you ever seen
a collection of miniature furniture to compare with

*"Mrs. Julian didn't come in today," Mr. Dance said,
guessing Cherry's thoughts*

this little dining-room set?" He held out a tray. On it were doll-size Chippendale chairs, table, and china closet of mahogany, set with tiny plates and silver coffeepots. "These were made for some fortunate child two hundred years ago."

"They're handsome, Mr. Dance. I'm afraid I don't know too much about art history, though."

She waited for him to supply some details about where and when these treasures had been made, by what craftsmen, and something about their style or authenticity. But Mr. Dance only said, "Beautiful, aren't they?"

"About Mrs. Julian—"

"Oh, she's a fine help to me. She has such an appreciation and knowledge of these things. Tell me, Miss Ames, she'll be all right, won't she? If you'd recommend shorter hours for her, or a brief vacation, or anything at all—"

"That's kind of you, Mr. Dance," Cherry said warmly. "Those are questions for a physician to answer. But so far as I could judge yesterday, Mrs. Julian is well. It's just that she has a high-strung temperament and any extra strain is hard on her."

Willard Dance nodded thoughtfully. "Yes, I know how keenly she feels everything. She tries so hard. This is her first job, you know—"

Adam Heller came up to them and cleared his throat, waiting for Dance's attention.

"Yes, Mr. Heller? By the way, this is our nurse, Miss Ames."

Cherry and the scholarly-looking old man exchanged how-do-you-do's.

"Excuse me for interrupting, Mr. Dance, but while you were upstairs Mr. Otto telephoned you. This is my first chance to tell you. I left a memo—"

"What, again! I've told Otto repeatedly not to phone me here!" Willard Dance was agitated. He shook his head and forced a smile. "Oh, that man, he never gives me any peace. Did he leave any message, Mr. Heller?"

"No, sir. He merely asked you to call him back."

"Well, thanks. Guess I'm touchy this morning. I slept very little last night."

Adam Heller nodded politely and walked away. Cherry stole a glance at the concessionaire. Dance certainly must be edgy to get so upset over a phone call. Well, Cherry decided, it was no concern of hers. Her job was in the medical department; she was staying away too long.

"If there's nothing further you want to ask me, Mr. Dance, I think I'd better be getting back."

"Wait, Miss Ames. There's something it might be well for you to understand about Anna Julian." He spoke with tact and care. "I myself am devoted to her. Concerned for her. Of course I value her in my business. But there are other reasons."

Mr. Dance went on to say that through his late wife he had become acquainted with the Julian family and knew how they had shielded their Anna Elizabeth from every practical worry. During her marriage her husband, too, had treated her as a child.

"You can imagine, Miss Ames, how unaccustomed it is for her to work for her living. Still, she has to, she has no financial resources except her job here, no one to turn to who can help her. She is completely alone in the world. Well"—Mr. Dance drew a deep breath "—that's why it's so very upsetting that Mrs. Julian is under suspicion of taking the Ming vase."

"But, Mr. Dance, surely you don't suspect her!"

"My dear Miss Ames, of course I don't! Am I not defending her against the store detectives and some of the executives who don't really know her?"

It began to dawn on Cherry that Mrs. Julian was really in trouble. She remembered one thing firmly in Mrs. Julian's favor.

"Mr. Dance, Mrs. Julian was investigated and accepted by a bonding company, wasn't she?"

"Yes, she was—*before* the Ming vase was stolen. She still is bonded, but the bonding company sent one of its investigators around here yesterday. The bonding company will be breathing hard down the back of her neck."

"I'm not sure I understand, Mr. Dance. I suppose

the store will have to pay in full for the value of the missing vase?"

"No, Miss Ames, I'm the one who is liable." He explained that although Thomas and Parke supplied routine protection service, his department was a separate, independent business within the store.

"But the vase was insured by its owner, wasn't it?" Cherry asked.

"Yes, the vase is insured by its owner. But whenever the owner of an insured object moves it to another location—for example, placing the vase on consignment here with me—the owner has to notify the insurance company. Once the vase is on my premises, I am responsible for it."

"I see. What a loss for you!"

"Well, I am insured, fortunately. Still, I don't want to have Anna Julian falsely accused. But what makes the situation harder—" Mr. Dance looked earnestly at her. "This is an awfully difficult thing to say, Miss Ames."

"I'll try to understand. And I'll regard it as confidential."

"Good. Well, you see, Anna Julian is, as you may have noticed, a rather emotional young woman. On the surface she is reserved, I grant you, but—possibly due to her inexperience of the world—sometimes she is *quite* emotional. She loses her self-control. Of course when one does that, one is—well, unreliable."

Cherry felt baffled. "Do I understand correctly? If she's unreliable at times, she *might* have taken the vase—is that it?"

"Oh, no, no, I'd prefer not to think such a thing! She's entirely well-meaning. All I'm saying, Miss Ames, is that she is, well, neurotic—that's the word, I suppose. Or overwrought. Or—I don't know." He looked unhappy.

Cherry gathered that Mr. Dance was warning her to take with a grain of salt whatever Mrs. Julian might tell her. That was odd. But what about *his* judgment? Was he painting an accurate picture of Anna Julian? Cherry decided she'd rather rely on her own knowledge of Mrs. Julian as she came to know her better.

"I just want you to treat her with extra consideration and patience," Mr. Dance said.

"I appreciate your telling me," Cherry replied. But she did not know what to make of this smiling, amiable, easygoing concessionaire. Cherry felt so torn by conflicting impressions that she was relieved to get away.

When she returned to her desk Cherry found a letter that had come in the morning's second mail delivery. Written on paper with the initials A.E.J., it read:

"Dear Miss Ames: After the Ming vase fiasco, I feel too exhausted to report to work on Tuesday. I am so sorry to miss our luncheon date, but can we postpone it to Thursday? Since Wednesday is my day off, I shall look forward to seeing you on Thursday at noon at the Mary White Restaurant.

Sincerely,
Anna Julian"

Reading the note, Cherry felt much better. At least this much of a rather unclear picture was cleared up.

Tomorrow she hoped to have a free day herself, to move with Gwen to Long Island. That is, if the personnel department would arrange it for her. Then the day after that, she would have lunch with Mrs. Julian.

Wednesday was a fine, clear, sunny day and Cherry and Gwen enjoyed the drive out to Long Island. The two friends rolled merrily along the landscaped parkways. They had packed clothes and nursing instruments and Gwen's pet gardenia plant in wild haste, answering all of the questions at No. 9 at the same time. Of course they'd visit the Spencer Club often! Of course the Spencer Club was invited out to Aunt Kathy's!

"Tell me something about your aunt," Cherry said, as Gwen drove.

"Not much to tell. She and Uncle John always wanted children, especially a daughter. And she's awfully nice."

She certainly was. Katherine Martin was youthful and lively, and though she probably was old enough to be the girls' mother, she neither looked nor acted it. She was lifting a large pasteboard box out of her own car in the driveway when the girls arrived.

"Eclairs," she explained. "If you don't like what's for lunch, we can feast on pastries. So you're Cherry! Hello! Gwen, darling, how are you? You two girls don't know how glad I am to have company. I just wish Uncle John could be here, too."

She led them into the house. Cherry noticed and liked the green plants growing everywhere in the Martins' house, and the piles of magazines and phonograph records, and when Aunt Kathy led them upstairs, the sunny bedrooms. Cherry's spacious room had bright maple furniture against Wedgwood-blue wallpaper.

"How delightful!" Cherry said. "You'll never be able to pry me out of this room."

"Yes, we will," said Aunt Kathy, "unless you never get hungry."

She explained that while her husband was abroad on business, she was giving the housekeeper a long-overdue vacation. "I thought the three of us wouldn't bother too much with housekeeping or meals in. There are so many good restaurants and lovely drives around here."

The first day passed rapidly. They gave Aunt Kathy their gift of perfume, demolished the eclairs, inspected the grounds, unpacked and changed, and by that time it was time to listen to the six-o'clock newscast. After dinner, all they did was listen to one television program and chat for a while. Then all of a sudden it was ten o'clock, and bedtime for the two commuters. Also, Cherry had a lunch date the next day with Mrs. Julian, and she wanted to feel fresh and alert for it.

Next morning's commuting was not at all bad. Everyone had warned her that the hour's ride would be tiresome, but Cherry amused herself by watching the other passengers on the train, and trying to guess what each one did. Did that tall, thin man lecture on learned subjects—or manufacture zippers? Was that assured blond girl a secretary or a fashion designer's assistant? Cherry noticed everyone was reading a morning newspaper. Having forgotten to purchase one at the station, she got to thinking of Anna Julian. Ever since Mr. Dance had emphasized yesterday how much she needed her job and how seriously she was under suspicion, Cherry felt a redoubled concern for Mrs. Julian. The woman's health could be seriously affected by anxiety.

That morning, while Nurse Gladys took care of the daily records, Cherry interviewed a salesgirl who came in complaining of severe headaches.

"They never go away, Miss Ames. I go to bed at night with a headache, and wake up next morning with a headache. I can't work properly; my supervisor has noticed, too."

She was a thin, rather drab girl, who looked older than her years. Her name was Dorothy Weiss, competent and reliable according to personnel reports, and her relations with store people were excellent. But her work was falling off.

"Have you been to an eye doctor?" Cherry asked. "Have you had a checkup by a physician?"

"Yes, I have, Miss Ames, and they tell me I seem to be all right. I took the prescribed medicine for headaches, but it helped only for a short time."

"Do you like your doctor, Miss Weiss? Do you have confidence in him and talk to him openly?"

"Well, to tell you the truth, I don't have any regular doctor whom I *know*. I went to my friend's doctor, just one visit. He was pretty rushed with some urgent cases the evening I was there."

"I see." Cherry knew from experience how hard-pressed and harried a doctor could be. Besides, a physical checkup did not always tell the whole story. "I wonder if you'd mind telling me something about your life outside of store hours?"

Dorothy Weiss said she had two brothers and two sisters, all married, with children and households of their own. Her father was dead; her mother, elderly and an invalid. Because Dorothy "had no other family responsibilities," the sisters and brothers said, she was left to support and nurse their mother. Her world consisted of working in the store, and at home, keeping house and nursing. Though neighbors looked in during the day, Dorothy hurried home on her lunch hour to give her mother necessary care. The girl was very tired, and nearly in despair.

"That's a hard situation," Cherry agreed sympathetically. "Do you think your brothers and sisters are being entirely fair?"

"Well, I'm too tired out to argue with them any more."

"What is your mother's illness?"

"Poor mother." Dorothy Weiss named a progressive disease. "It's incurable."

"But it isn't!" Cherry exclaimed. "That is, it was until two or three months ago, but a cure has been discovered. I read about it in a medical journal. It isn't known to the general public yet—"

"A cure? Are you sure, Miss Ames?"

"Yes! They are *using* the new techniques at New York Hospital with good results. Why don't you go there and—"

Cherry recommended that Miss Weiss go to the clinic there for advice. If her mother was too ill to come to the hospital, the hospital would send a doctor, and if hospital treatment was advisable, an ambu-

lance. The costs would be scaled to what Dorothy
Weiss could afford.

The girl's face lighted up with hope, a cautious
hope. In the strong daylight Cherry saw she could
be a pretty girl—and lose those headaches, given half
a chance.

"Now I want to tell you about the visiting nurses,"
Cherry said. "It's an hourly nursing service. They're
registered nurses—I was a visiting nurse myself."

As Cherry described how a visiting nurse would
come in and care for the mother, the girl's eyes grew
wider and brighter.

Cherry planned a daily routine with her, allowing the girl some free time for herself. Cherry suggested, too, some simplified housekeeping routines
and quick tricks which she had learned while a private duty nurse.

"Why, Miss Ames, I feel as if I'm getting part way
out of prison! I'll tell you something—I have hardly
any headache now."

Cherry felt rewarded. It was a good morning's
work—"even if I don't have another patient this
morning!"

Cherry did have one more patient before lunch
hour. It was Santa Claus from the toy department,
a fat man, made even fatter with pillows. He actually
staggered in.

"Nurse," he said, half grumbling, half laughing,

"those kids will be the death of me. My head is splitting."

"Sit down, Santa," Cherry said. "And don't bother to waggle your beard at *me*."

She gave him an aspirin tablet with a glass of water, and let him rest and grumble.

"Listen, has anyone asked Santa what *he* wants for Christmas? I'll tell you what I want! More Santa Clauses, and in a hurry. I can't hold this fort alone in the toy department, not with the mobs that're already coming in."

Cherry made a mental note to mention the request to Tom Reese. A few minutes later Santa Claus, looking relieved, went back to the toy department.

And now it was time for Cherry to keep her luncheon appointment with Mrs. Julian. Up until now she had not admitted to herself how eager and curious she was for this interview. Cherry changed into street clothes, and then thought if Mrs. Julian was ready, they could leave the store together.

"I haven't seen her all morning," said Miss Janet Lamb to Cherry. "I presume she's upstairs." The store detectives' office was on the seventh and top floor; that meant more questioning. "Yes, certainly, Miss Ames, I'll tell Mrs. Julian you're on your way to meet her."

The Mary White Restaurant was crowded at noon hour, but Cherry had taken the precaution of telephoning for a reservation. The hostess showed her to a table for two, which was, thank goodness, in a quiet corner so they could talk.

Cherry waited. Five minutes, ten minutes, fifteen. She watched the door for Mrs. Julian, but the woman did not come in. Finally, after twenty minutes of sitting alone and feeling foolish, Cherry ordered lunch. This was Mrs. Julian's second failure to show up. It made Cherry uneasy. Did the woman *not* want to tell her anything further? Or was she, as Mr. Dance had warned, simply an unreliable, unpredictable person? Couldn't she at least have sent a message that she couldn't come?

After her solitary lunch, Cherry returned to the store and went directly to the antiques department. There was Mrs. Julian!

She was just finishing with a customer, who was leisurely chatting. Mrs. Julian caught Cherry's eyes and barely perceptibly shrugged her shoulders, as if to say, "I can't hurry her along, you see." Cherry, trying to be patient, waited until the customer left.

Anna Julian came hurrying over to Cherry. She looked better today after some rest, her simple black silk dress set off her fair hair and clear blue eyes.

"Miss Ames, I'm so very sorry I couldn't meet you for lunch. I didn't even have a minute to let you know! Please forgive me. I was rude, through no fault of my own."

"Not at all," Cherry murmured, half won over by Mrs. Julian's earnestness.

"It's simply that I had customers all through lunch hour. Mr. Dance especially asked me to take care of them. First a man who wanted to see some of our antique fans, and then Mrs. James, whom you saw. I couldn't very well refuse Mr. Dance's request. I am most awfully sorry, Miss Ames, I do apologize."

Cherry smiled at her, thinking, no, Mrs. Julian couldn't refuse to do what her employer asked.

At that moment Willard Dance appeared from around the edge of the wall-size tapestry which apparently concealed his office.

"Did Mrs. James buy a table, Mrs. Julian? Which one?"

"Yes, she took the round rosewood table, Mr. Dance."

"Good for you! A very nice sale, Mrs. Julian! Hello, Miss Ames. Now you see how skillful our Mrs. Julian is. That Mrs. James is a charming woman, but difficult."

As usual, the concessionaire was beaming and affable, caressing the rosewood table with his finger tips.

"You haven't had lunch yet, have you?" Dance said to Mrs. Julian. "Why don't you go now? In fact, why don't you take the afternoon off? You spent a hard morning upstairs."

"Oh, no, Mr. Dance, thanks just the same. The Foxes are coming in this afternoon to select a rug. It will be a big sale, and I should be here."

"Well, if you change your mind—" And Mr. Dance turned away to answer his ringing telephone.

Now that Cherry and Mrs. Julian were alone together, the woman sighed and sat down on a bench.

"I'm not feeling very well," she admitted. "I realize it's mostly worry and nervousness, being under suspicion about the Ming vase, more than anything physical. I can't sleep. I haven't slept a night through since the vase disappeared."

Cherry suggested things to do to relieve insomnia; a warm, not hot bath before bedtime, a glass of warm milk. "Some people enjoy reading in bed or listening to music from a bedside radio. It frees their minds from the day's worries."

Mrs. Julian smiled. "My dear, are you trying to tell me I mustn't worry about the Ming vase? That's very good of you. Do you suppose I might stop addressing you formally and call you Cherry?"

Cherry was pleased. When Mrs. Julian asked to be called Anna, Cherry shook her head. "You're not *much* older than I am, but you're firmly fixed in my mind as Mrs. Julian. I couldn't any more do that than I could call Mr. Dance by his first name."

"I can't call him Willard, either," Anna Julian confided. "Come over here and see the gorgeous necklace he purchased abroad. He's had it at his apartment ever since he was abroad last year. He says he'd hoped to find a private customer for it. Evidently he didn't, because here it is." She led Cherry to a locked display case.

The necklace was of rose diamonds, gems of graduated sizes, set in an intricate design, ending in a medallion which was a burst of fire and color. Cherry had never seen anything so magnificent.

"It must be worth a fortune. It's worthy of a museum, isn't it, Mrs. Julian?"

"Unless I'm mistaken, it was designed and made in Vienna about 1800. Probably it belonged to a member of the royal family. I remember seeing jewels in similar designs when my family took me to Vienna as a girl. You notice the rather heavy, clumsy workmanship, which is beautiful in its own way— and the baroque spray designs circling each large diamond. That's how you place its date and origin."

"Doesn't Mr. Dance know its history?" Cherry asked. "After all, he bought it."

Mrs. Julian made a face. "Mr. Dance doesn't pretend to know much art history. He says so bluntly. Not that I mean that as a criticism! He is a capable and experienced businessman, and *so* kind to me."

"Don't forget that your knowledge of antiques is valuable to him, too."

"Yes, Cherry, but who else would keep me on,

on my job, after an ugly affair like the Ming vase theft? More than that, Mr. Dance says I can rely on him to help clear my good name, because he is vouching to the detectives for my good character."

Cherry had not the heart to say she doubted if that would be enough to clear Mrs. Julian. Besides, the store detectives, city police, and insurance detectives were working on the case and they would require more proof than Mr. Dance's word. Tom Reese had hinted as much.

"There's one thing I don't understand," Mrs. Julian said musingly, "although I trust Willard Dance beyond question. Since he is determined to retain me on his staff, and since he's promised to clear me, why hasn't he taken *action* to clear me? The store detectives, particularly Mr. Pierce, when they questioned me this morning, said nothing about Mr. Dance's statement on my behalf."

"Yes, it is hard to understand," Cherry commented warily.

"Still, perhaps he hasn't found the propitious moment to speak up for me. I'm sure he will; he promised."

Mrs. Julian steered the conversation back to the rose diamond necklace, and some of the rare and beautiful furniture. Cherry's enjoyment of these things gave Mrs. Julian real pleasure.

"You know, Cherry, I have a few small treasures

of my own. Nothing as grand and costly as the things here, but still, I would like you to see them. Will you come for tea this Sunday at my apartment?"

"Why—why—I'd love to! Thank you so much, Mrs. Julian."

Nothing could have pleased Cherry more, for it proved she had won the young woman's confidence, and it might perhaps give her a chance to help Anna Julian in some way.

"At five this Sunday, then," said Mrs. Julian, and gave Cherry her address.

CHAPTER V

Mr. Otto and the Music Box

THE FIRST PERSON CHERRY SAW THE NEXT MORN-
ing when she arrived at the sixth floor was Tom
Reese.

"Happy new month," he said. Today, Friday, was
the first of December. "Also Merry Christmas," he
said. "I want to break the news to you that starting
today, we'll be open until nine every evening until
Christmas. No more days off, either, young lady. You
and your assistant had better arrange split schedules
between you. You'll have to work some evenings."

"Yes, sir! Yes, sir! I'll requisition an extra cot,
too. Speaking of a Merry Christmas, could you
please give our toy department's Santa Claus a present?" She told Tom Reese about the man's earnest
wish for additional Santas.

Tom grinned and said he'd relay the request to

the personnel department. "I saw you talking with Mrs. Julian yesterday. How's she standing up under the strain of cross-examination?"

"It isn't easy for her. By the way, she's asked me to tea at her house this Sunday."

"Oh? That's nice."

Tom Reese's dark eyes sparkled exactly as Cherry's did. She wondered if Tom realized he and she looked so much alike that some passing employees stared at them.

"Well, Cherry, don't let the Christmas rush get you down. Maybe I'll see you sooner than you think," he said mysteriously and dashed away.

That set the pace. It was hectic. With more employees being hired, with more shoppers pouring into the store, Cherry had plenty to do.

"Lunch?" said Tom Reese, popping in at noon.

"The Christmas *rush* seems to be you," Cherry said, laughing.

"Well, besides wanting to have lunch with you, I'd like to talk with you about Anna Julian. If she's invited you to her house, you must be getting to know her pretty well."

Over sandwiches in the employees' cafeteria, they tried to think out what they could do together to help Mrs. Julian.

"I'd like to save her job for her, if I can," Tom said. "If she loses her position here, she won't secure another one easily. Not with the suspicion of theft hanging over her."

"There's one hopeful angle." Cherry recalled, and repeated Mrs. Julian's remark that Mr. Dance did not know too much about antiques. Considering that he operated the gallery, he should be well informed on the subject. "Isn't that reason enough for Mr. Dance to need Mrs. Julian's expert knowledge, and keep her on?"

"Yes, I should think so." He added that, at Mr. Dance's insistence, she would not be questioned any more this week.

Cherry hesitated, then asked Tom a question which was bothering her. "Tell me honestly, does the store seriously suspect Mrs. Julian, or is she imagining some of it?" Or, Cherry added to herself, is Mr. Dance exaggerating it?

"It's a real and serious suspicion, Cherry. Some of the executives, and at least one of the store detectives, Hal Pierce, are convinced Mrs. Julian is the thief. Pierce swears he's going to prove it. Some of them wanted to fire her at once, but they've agreed she can be observed and questioned better if she remains in the store."

Tom Reese explained that the insurance company detectives were doing most of the investigating, because it was the insurance company that was losing money on the Ming vase. Tom added that the insurance company's detective service was a much bigger operation than the store's service, limited to this building. The insurance company had a few detectives whom they sent all over the United States, in case the thief had taken or sent the vase to another city. And they worked closely with city police.

"With all those men on the job," Cherry asked, "have they located any clue to the vase?"

"No. Perhaps I should say not yet. Anyway, not all criminals are caught. A gay lunch we're having, hey?"

"I can't feel very gay with that poor woman in trouble," Cherry said. "Maybe I should be suspicious of her, but a theft is so—so out of character for her."

"Well, it might be a good idea to keep our minds open. Keep our eyes and ears open, too, and do a mild sort of sleuthing," Tom said cheerfully.

So Tom was going to try, too, to help Mrs. Julian! He was in a unique position to do so. He was assistant to the store manager, and the store's protection department—the detectives—reported directly to the store manager. Cherry felt very glad that she had had this lunch with him, and this talk.

Because Tom was in a terrific hurry as usual, Cherry had fifteen minutes of her lunch hour left, so she decided to stop at the antiques department.

Mrs. Julian was there, and free at the moment to talk. She looked haggard.

"You didn't sleep again last night?" Cherry guessed.

Mrs. Julian shrugged. "I've lost five pounds since the vase disappeared."

"You're too slim to lose weight. Perhaps you should see a doctor."

"Even the best doctor couldn't dispel this dark cloud of suspicion. Oh, let's change the subject. Cherry, I want to show you a marvelous highboy that just arrived!"

She led Cherry across the department, but Mrs. James with her poodle tucked under her arm stopped her.

"Mrs. Julian, I want to ask you about the history of the rosewood table I purchased."

"Certainly, Mrs. James. I did start to tell you, didn't I?"

Mr. Dance, overhearing, came up to say that eight matching rosewood chairs might be available soon, if an estate were settled and offered for sale. He nodded to Cherry as Mrs. Julian moved off with her customer. To be pleasant, Cherry said:

"Mrs. Julian was about to show me a highboy she's excited about."

"We're all thrilled with it. Just look at it, Miss Ames!"

They paused before a simple and magnificent highboy which stood nearly seven feet high. Massive, of gleaming mahogany, it easily outshone anything else in the gallery.

"Just look at the shell carving at the top!" Mr. Dance drew Cherry's attention to the highboy's fine points: the exact matching of the wood's grain, the ease with which the capacious drawers slid open, the fine brass handles, the gracefully turned legs. It had been made in the early eighteenth century, entirely by hand, by a Rhode Island master craftsman for a wealthy sea captain. He had taken it in his clipper ship to China where he sold it to a mandarin for a fortune in jewels.

"So Mrs. Julian tells me," Mr. Dance said. "The highboy has a long, involved history. I don't recall everything Mrs. Julian said. It's nearly priceless."

Only three such highboys were made. One was in England, privately owned, one was missing, and here was the third.

"These old craftsmen were artists." Cherry was full of admiration. "How do you ever know where to locate such treasures, Mr. Dance?"

He stroked his balding head in a pleased sort of way. "In this field it's important to know people who collect antiques, and it's important for them to know about me. So that, Miss Ames, when someone has a highboy or a vase he wishes to sell, he brings it to me, and I try to sell it for him. Now, take this wonderful highboy—a man's who's just closed his big house, a famous art collector, sent it to me."

"It doesn't belong to you, then?" Cherry asked.

"I only wish it were mine. No, Miss Ames, it's here on loan—on consignment, the usual arrangement, a percentage to me if I can sell it— Otto! When did you get here?"

"You have no time to talk to Otto?" said a heavy voice.

A man brushed past Cherry and forced her aside. She was astonished. What arrogance! She stared at the tall, paunchy, bulletheaded man, and disliked him for his overbearing rudeness.

"So, my friend, the famous highboy has arrived." Mr. Otto turned his back on Cherry. "You are so sure it is authentic?" His voice rang with mockery. "You don't mislead your customers?"

"Examine it, Otto," said Dance deferentially. "I'm awfully glad you could come in today. I'd like you to have a look at the rose diamond necklace as well, and have your opinion."

Mr. Otto began to talk to Mr. Dance about the technicalities of antiques. Apparently he was a specialist in this field, active as a consultant to Willard Dance. Wasn't Mr. Otto the one whose telephone calls Dance had complained about? Perhaps, Cherry thought, Dance was just upset that morning because of the theft of the vase. The two men seemed to know each other fairly well.

"Mr. Dance, Mr. Otto," said Anna Julian, trying to get a word in edgewise, "if you could give me some idea about those rosewood chairs— Mrs. James has left but wants me to notify her."

"Don't interrupt, if you please!" Otto dismissed her.

"Later, my dear." Willard Dance smiled over his shoulder. He returned his full attention to Mr. Otto, who opened an oversized brief case. The case was big and important-looking, and the man carried it as if it were his badge of office.

Mrs. Julian plucked Cherry's sleeve and urged her away from the two preoccupied men. "What a character!" Cherry muttered under her breath.

"Yes—well—let's talk of something pleasanter," Mrs. Julian said. "You've seen the highboy?"

They strolled back for another look at the magnificent chest.

"If it's such a rarity," Cherry remarked, "it's a wonder the store isn't being mobbed by art collectors and museum directors, trying to purchase it."

Anna Julian smiled. "You're quite right. We would be mobbed if people knew the highboy was here. As a matter of fact, Adam Heller told me not ten minutes ago that the highboy has been sold."

"Already! I don't understand."

"Yes, the highboy came in only this morning. But that's not too unusual—"

Mrs. Julian explained to Cherry that in this business art dealers favored certain steady customers, giving them first chance to purchase rarities. It was evident Mr. Dance had notified a preferred customer the instant the highboy had been delivered this morning, and the customer had snapped it up.

"I understand," Mrs. Julian added, "that a private collector—not a museum or estate—has purchased the highboy. I don't know his name. Mr. Dance hasn't said. You know, this is a famous highboy and there could be an awful lot of publicity about its changing hands—newspaper inquiries and photographers wanting to come to the customer's house. It would be a nuisance to the customer, and Mr. Dance doesn't want to embarrass him. Later, when the highboy is actually delivered to him, I'm sure the new owner will send a publicity statement to the newspapers and art magazines about his acquisition. Probably soon. It *is* news."

As Mrs. Julian talked, Cherry watched Mr. Otto examine an old American painting, inch by inch, under a magnifying glass. Otto might be expert, but he certainly was an unpleasant man.

The week end, fortunately, was pleasanter than the tensions Cherry had been dealing with in the store. Early Saturday evening, after a hectic day's work, she arrived at the Long Island house to find it

Cherry watched Mr. Otto examine an old American painting

full of girls. All the lights were blazing, music filled the living room, and the Spencer Club was in full swing. Aunt Kathy, passing tomato-juice cocktails and canapés, said:

"Don't look so surprised, Cherry. You know we're having a house party this week end."

"Guess I forgot, Aunt Kathy. I've been up to my ears in work all day. How are you all? How's No. 9? Vivian, what a becoming dress!" Vivian flushed with pleasure. After Vivian's long struggle to earn her own way, a new dress was still an occasion.

"Our fashion plate," Bertha said with good-humored envy. Bertha was plump from her own good farm-style cooking, and never cared what she wore.

"We waited for you, Cherry, at Pennsylvania Station," said Mai Lee. "We let three trains pass, thinking you'd be along any minute."

Cherry thanked her friends and said, "If you knew what that medical department is like on a Saturday—especially before Christmas. That's why I'm late."

"The late Miss Ames," Gwen chanted.

Aunt Kathy called them all into the dining room for a buffet supper. She was amused by their chatter and by the amounts of refreshments they could consume.

"We're eating you out of house and home, Mrs. Martin," said Mai Lee.

"Never mind. I haven't had so much fun since I

was a girl. Only I have never, never heard so much nursing talk in my life!"

Their talking continued far into Saturday night. Aunt Kathy had stowed them away, as Gwen put it, two or three girls to each bedroom. Naturally the six girls did not stay put; all of them congregated in Gwen's room. At midnight Aunt Kathy sleepily came in.

"Since nobody is going to bed, let's go downstairs and fix ourselves fried-egg sandwiches or something."

Having stayed up half the night shortened Sunday considerably. If Cherry hadn't had an appointment in town with Mrs. Julian, she might not have gotten up until the middle of next week. Nursing was hard, tiring work, no matter how rewarding it could be. Cherry showered, dressed, and found the rest of the sleepy household glowering at her for her virtuous example. Besides, in her zeal, she had a couple of hours left until train time. Cherry filled it by writing letters home. She wasn't sure what she was writing, what with everyone coming and going and chattering around her. But she expected her family would forgive any incoherence.

In contrast to this jamboree, Mrs. Julian's apartment was startlingly quiet.

Anna Julian met her at the door, looking more nearly Cherry's age than she did in the store. Perhaps because she had spent her childhood mostly in

Europe and mostly with adults, she had a settled, dignified manner which contrasted with her glowing youth. She wore a softer dress and coiffure, but more than that, Cherry noticed, her expression was pensive and a little anxious—as if, at home, she need not keep up pretenses.

"You're very nice to make a special trip to visit me," Mrs. Julian remarked as she led Cherry into the living room.

Cherry had half expected to see another visitor or two, but they were alone. A mantel clock ticked loudly in the stillness of the room. The clock was of porcelain, and so was the tea service which Mrs. Julian had ready on a tole tray. Every furnishing of the small room was chosen with an eye to beauty.

"What lovely things you have!" Cherry exclaimed, although she was appalled by the air of loneliness in here. It was an apartment scaled down to the needs of one solitary tenant. One armchair. One reading lamp. One chair drawn up beside the radio.

"I had many more things which you would have liked," Mrs. Julian said as she gave Cherry a cup of steaming jasmine tea. "But after my husband died—or rather, during his long illness—I disposed of most of our household."

Cherry did not want to dwell on a topic which must be painful for Anna Julian. She changed the subject.

"Are you from New York originally, Mrs. Julian?"

"No, my family lived in San Francisco, though we were often in New York en route to Europe. Ralph, my husband, was a San Francisco man. We lived there at first after our marriage. We—we came to New York in search of medical care for him."

And now he was dead, and her family was dead. Cherry tried to be tactful. "San Francisco must be a fabulous city. I've always wanted to see it."

"Yes, it's wonderful, but I don't ever want to return there."

Too many memories? Cherry tried again, saying that her Middle West was pretty wonderful, too, in its own way. But Mrs. Julian *wanted* to talk about her husband.

"You see, Cherry, Ralph had a rare form of cancer which was not operable. For a long time he didn't even realize he was ill because, though he sometimes complained of not feeling right, he stubbornly refused to have a medical checkup. So busy with business—Ralph had a fine shop which sold musical instruments—and besides, he rather dreaded admitting that he *might* be ill. Playing ostrich, I used to tell him. He wouldn't listen. You as a nurse must know—"

Cherry nodded. "Delay is the most dangerous thing people can do. So many diseases, even cancer, are curable *providing* the patient comes in the early stages for treatment. If only people would be sensible and have an annual health checkup! They take their cars to the garage periodically, but neglect themselves."

Mrs. Julian's husband had neglected himself to the point where his condition became serious. They exhausted the medical resources of their city, then they were advised to try the foremost cancer research center and hospital in the nation, located in the East. Ralph Julian sold his business, and with these funds and with what Mrs. Julian had inherited from her parents' mismanaged estate, they moved to New York City.

"We were cheerful. We thought Ralph would be cured in a year or less, and able to work again. But his condition deteriorated. We had enough to live on for two years and pay medical bills, too."

The husband's illness dragged on for four years. Cherry understood how this must have eaten into their resources. No wonder Mrs. Julian had sold most of their household furnishings at such a time.

"I nursed him," Mrs. Julian went on, "and tried to maintain a cheerful home. The hospital was wonderful. Even for Ralph's rare form of cancer they had techniques. The doctors did everything humanly possible. But he had waited too long."

Cherry tried to think of something to say. But what could anyone say? Luckily, Mrs. Julian was much too self-contained and much too well-mannered to indulge in tears or self-pity or too personal confidences. She rose to show Cherry the porcelain clock.

"Ralph gave me this for our first anniversary present. My mother had told him how I had fallen in love with it at a gallery, and he was wildly extravagant. I'm so glad he was."

"And this tea service?"

"Oh, I gave my husband that for his birthday, one year," Mrs. Julian said and burst out laughing. "Fortunately I gave him something else that he wanted, too. A pen, I think."

"Here's my proudest possession, Cherry," and Mrs. Julian lifted from a table an old-fashioned wooden music box, hand-painted with a garland of flowers. It was fairly large and bulky, though it rested comfortably in Cherry's two outstretched hands. Mrs. Julian wound the handle, lifted the lid, and the notched metal plate began to spin.

A light and peculiarly touching melody issued from the music box. It was a plaintive minuet, with an odd fall of notes. Cherry listened closely, and when the melody was repeated, she hummed along with it.

"It's lovely! Will you play it again?"

"Of course." Mrs. Julian wound the music box. Cherry listened delightedly again, all the way through, every note speaking to her like a voice.

A voice from long ago, for Mrs. Julian said the music box had been made a century and a half ago in Germany. "It belonged to a little princess, if you please. There isn't another music box like it. I checked on that. Willard Dance was quite entranced with it when he visited me."

They talked about that endlessly interesting subject, the department store, and were beginning to discuss the missing Ming vase, when at six o'clock the doorbell rang.

"He's punctual!" Mrs. Julian exclaimed.

Cherry did not know whom to expect. She was flabbergasted when Tom Reese walked in, and very pleased.

"Hello, Cherry. Awfully sweet of you to let me come, Mrs. Julian." Tom looked too strong and active for this room, full of breakables. He sat down on an antique chair and Cherry prayed that it would hold him. "Cherry, I might as well admit it. When I found out you were coming here this afternoon, I up and asked Mrs. Julian to invite me, too."

"Such gallantry," Cherry murmured, feeling her cheeks burn.

"Well," Tom said bluntly, "I don't know you well enough to ask you for a date, and I'll never get to know you at work, not in all that rush. So—" He gestured and the chair creaked.

"As long as we're being candid," said Mrs. Julian,

"would you mind sitting on the couch, Mr. Reese? It is sturdier."

They all laughed, and Tom beamed at Cherry. She hadn't realized he liked her, particularly; Tom was so friendly to everyone in the store. However, Cherry surmised that there was another reason for his calling on Mrs. Julian today. Tom must be trying to tell her that he, at least, among the store executives, regarded her as above suspicion.

"I'm sorry you couldn't come earlier," Mrs. Julian said to Tom.

"Thanks, but you know I go away every week end, right after work on Saturdays." He said that he went with two other young men to the Connecticut home of the parents of one of them.

They chatted for a while. Half an hour later Tom stood up and said it was time for him to go. He seemed to be waiting for Cherry to come along, but Cherry did not wish to abandon her hostess. She couldn't very well suggest dinner; that was up to the man of the party, and Tom was frowning at his wrist watch.

"What are your plans for this evening, Mrs. Julian?" Cherry asked.

"I'm going to church, to seven-o'clock service. Then I think I'll stroll home, and go to bed early for a long night's rest—Miss Nurse."

"Very wise of you. Will you excuse me, then?

And thank you so much for the delightful tea party."

"I enjoyed having you," Mrs. Julian said warmly.

"You're an angel, Anna Julian," Tom stated as he followed Cherry out of the apartment.

He had his car parked downstairs, but Tom confessed that he had to do desk work for most of this evening.

"Anyway, I can drive you home," he insisted. "Work, work, work, that's all we do! During the Christmas shopping season, at any rate. What are you doing Christmas Eve? The rush will be over by then."

"It's a date," Cherry promised.

"I'll see you before that!"

They had a long, lovely drive home.

CHAPTER VI

A Most Ingenious Trick

"THIS PLACE," CHERRY DECLARED TO GLADYS ON Monday, "looks like a schoolroom! You'd think we were entertaining the first grade."

They had their hands full with misplaced and banged-up children. The small boy lying on the cot had a nosebleed, brought on by the excitement of meeting Santa Claus. Cherry had just stanched the flow with a compress of medicated cotton and had sent to the store cafeteria for a little lemon juice for him to drink. The boy's mother approved the lemon juice, which was an old-fashioned, effective measure, but felt Cherry should summon a doctor.

"Madam," said Cherry, trying to be patient, "the bleeding has stopped, you can see for yourself. Let Bobby rest a bit, then if you wish you can take him to a doctor."

"I ain't goin' to any nasty old doctor," Bobby growled.

"Ssh! Nurse, are you *sure* Bobby is going to be all right?"

"Yes, he didn't lose very much blood."

"I did, too!" Bobby protested. "I lost as much blood as Tiger Injun in that movie where he nearly gets killed!"

"Ah, that was probably catsup and not blood at all," said Cherry. She turned to Bobby's mother. "I don't mean to minimize the tiring aftereffects of nosebleed. I'd suggest you take Bobby directly home in a few minutes, and have him rest. He may need a little extra nourishment, too—for example, a chocolate soda before you start on the ride home."

"Yippee!" Tiger Injun bounced up on the cot.

"You're supposed to be lying down, in ambush," and Cherry made him lie flat on his back again.

"I'll be your lookout scout," his mother promised, and let Cherry leave.

In the medical department's main room, small children of various shapes and sizes were perched here and there, nursing a banged, bandaged finger, or, in the case of two tiny girls, howling for their "lost" mother.

Cherry was attending to the small girls when all of a sudden the children shouted with glee.

"Santa Claus!" they said blissfully, pointing.

Cherry turned around and there stood the fugitive from the toy department.

"Headache again?" Cherry inquired.

"Santa Claus!" Several small voices rose in a clamor and Bobby came running in to see. "Bring me a sled, Santa!" "I want a talking doll, Santy!" "Look-it me, Santa—"

"Never mind," said Santa Claus to the nurse. "Just give me an aspirin!"

After the peak hours of afternoon shopping, the store hospital quieted down. Tuesday was relatively quiet. Cherry was congratulating herself when, Tuesday afternoon, the telephone rang.

"Medical department, Miss Ames speaking."

"Cherry, this is Tom Reese." He sounded unusually excited. "There's been a second theft. The highboy has been stolen."

"That enormous chest? But that's fantastic."

"Yes, but it's true. You know Mrs. Julian fairly well, maybe you can be of use to me. Can you come at once?"

"I'll be right there."

Cherry hung up, adjusted her crisp white cap straighter on her black curls, and went next door. She had never been in Tom Reese's private office before. His heaped-up desk interested her, with its roughs of store advertisements, shipping schedules, personnel reports, credit ratings, correspondence.

"Everything except merchandising," he said, following her glance, "comes under the jurisdiction of the store manager. Sit down, Cherry. This is bad business."

"For Mrs. Julian, too?"

"Yes. I'll come right to the point with you. The highboy has just been stolen, and about ten days ago the miniature Ming vase was stolen. The store detectives suspected Anna Julian of taking the vase, so now they figure she may be connected with the second antiques theft. Pierce, in particular, argues that it's no coincidence both thefts occurred in Mrs. Julian's department."

"Tom, do you think Anna Julian has stolen anything? Though how anyone could steal such an immense, well-known—"

"Well, listen to this trick. Let's see what you think."

The highboy was sold last Friday, as Cherry already knew. Mr. Dance had released the buyer's name to the delivery-service department, so that the highboy could be delivered at once to a Fifth Avenue address. The highboy was delivered last Saturday, and the store's deliverymen reported nothing unusual, except that the house was scantily furnished.

But this morning, Tuesday morning, the credit department reported that a check given in part payment for the highboy, a small deposit, had been

returned by the bank as worthless. The highboy was
charged to the customer's account, a perfectly good
account. The store detectives immediately sent men
to the Fifth Avenue address. They found the house
vacant and untenanted. The valuable highboy was
gone. What happened, apparently, was that the house
was rented temporarily and the highboy was removed to some unknown hiding place.

"So the Fifth Avenue address was simply a re-
spectable 'front,' is that it?" Cherry asked. "Who
was the customer who'd do such a thing?"

"We contacted the customer. He was astounded—
said he never ordered the highboy, although Mr.
Dance had phoned him it was available."

"Is the customer telling the truth?" Cherry asked.

"Well, he's a man whose reputation is beyond
question. Have you seen the name John Cleveland
in the newspapers as one of the President's dollar-
a-year men and heading up Red Cross committees?"

Cherry nodded. The name was a respected one.

Although the highboy was charged to Mr. John
Cleveland's long-standing and perfectly sound account, Tom explained, it was done by an agent. Or
by a man *claiming* to represent Mr. Cleveland, with
authority to act for him. The so-called agent purchased the highboy and ordered it sent not to Mr.
Cleveland's address but to the Fifth Avenue address,
saying Mr. Cleveland was sending it as a gift to his

daughter. But Mr. Cleveland declared today that he had no agent, that he had not authorized any such purchase, and that his daughter lived in Virginia.

"So the agent was an impostor," Cherry said, "and the Fifth Avenue address was a phony setup. How could Willard Dance have been fooled like that?"

"Easy enough. We questioned Dance at noon today," Tom said. "Dance says the agent offered him written credentials with John Cleveland's signature. Faked and forged, of course, but Dance says these were good enough to convince him. No, it's not Dance's fault. Busy, prominent people like Mr. Cleveland often send an agent to transact business for them. The 'agent' was awfully clever, that's all."

Cherry sat staring at Tom Reese as he picked at a knotted string, stubbornly trying to untangle it. She had never before seen him fidgety and angry.

"About the check that bounced—?"

"That's what alerted our bookkeeping and credit departments," Tom said. "It was the phony agent who gave a rubber check, in part payment for the highboy—to expedite its immediate delivery. He charged the balance to John Cleveland, claiming he was authorized to do so."

So in exchange for a worthless check, the unknown man had obtained possession of the highboy.

"Has the store any idea who the 'agent' was?" Cherry asked.

"No. Dance furnished a detailed description of the man, and detectives are now hunting for him. Dance is contacting other art dealers, including Mr. Otto who knows a lot of people, to see whether they know the 'agent.' But locating him or the highboy in a city of this size is—"

"Like searching for a needle in a haystack," Cherry said. "What else did Mr. Dance say?"

Mr. Dance had told store executives and detectives that on Friday morning, when the highboy arrived in the store, he telephoned the John Cleveland residence. Mr. Cleveland did not come to the telephone; Dance spoke to a secretary, presumably. He left a message that the famed highboy was for sale, in case Mr. Cleveland wanted first chance to acquire it. Thus, Willard Dance had said, he was not surprised when a little later on Friday a man claiming to represent Mr. Cleveland came to buy the highboy. When the 'agent' said that the prominent Mr. Cleveland wished no publicity about his acquisition just yet, Willard Dance honored the request. It was usual enough—and Cherry recalled Mrs. Julian's confirming that.

"I must say," Tom admitted, "that Mr. Cleveland is being awfully decent. He's already let our detectives search his New York house, and he's offered to throw open his country home for search."

"Tom," said Cherry musingly, "do you think

Willard Dance is telling the truth? All we have is his word for what happened."

"Yes, I believe him. His story is airtight. And he's badly worried. Because he's the one who sustains the loss of the highboy. *Dance* is the one whom the phony agent victimized—"

"Not the store? Besides, I thought Dance was insured."

"Look, Cherry, it works like this—"

Tom impatiently flung away the knotted string and explained. Actually there was no money loss to the store. The store could not charge Mr. Cleveland for an article which he neither ordered nor received. The charge for the highboy would simply be deleted from his account. Nor did the "agent's" bad check cost the store any money. Mr. Dance sustained the loss of the bad check, since his concession—his independent business—accepted it. What was lost, so far as the store was concerned, was the highboy itself, and this was Mr. Dance's responsibility.

"Wasn't it insured?" Cherry asked.

"Dance *had* been insured, but after the Ming vase was stolen, his insurance company considered him guilty of carelessness, a poor risk. They paid on the Ming vase, but they canceled his policy on the usual five days' notice. Dance just told me this." Tom frowned. "He's trying to get further insurance from another company."

"But the highboy—wasn't it insured earlier by its owner?"

Tom explained. When the owner transferred the highboy from his house to Dance's antiques gallery within the store, he notified his own insurance company of the highboy's change of location. Once the highboy was on Dance's premises, Dance was responsible for it. The owner's insurance company now held Willard Dance responsible to pay back to them the full value of the missing highboy—many thousands of dollars. The insurance company in turn would pay this sum to the highboy's owner, who had taken out and paid for the insurance policy.

"What is Dance going to do?" Cherry exclaimed.

Tom shrugged. "He's remarkably calm in the face of trouble. What we all hope is that the missing items can be found. Dance claims he's been victimized, and he's asking the owner's insurance company to give him a little time to let him co-operate with their detectives. But they're not giving him much time—one to two weeks, not more. Insurance companies are tough, Cherry. I think they said Dance has to pay right after Christmas—unless the highboy is located, or the thief is caught and confesses where the missing things are."

"You say 'the things,' " Cherry observed, "as if you almost think the same thief took both the vase and the highboy."

"*I* don't think so. I don't know what to think, at this stage," Tom replied. "Some of the detectives said that. They believe both thefts were an inside job."

"By someone like Mrs. Julian?" Cherry asked unwillingly. "But, Tom, why Mrs. Julian? Why not another insider like Miss Janet Lamb or Adam Heller or even Mr. Dance himself?"

"Because of all those people, only Mrs. Julian is without any family or any resources except her job. She's the only one in Dance's department who has real motive to steal. That's why the police detectives, with store and insurance company detectives, are inclined to suspect her."

"Does Mr. Dance suspect her, now that the highboy has disappeared?"

Tom shook his head. "Still, everyone is suspect until proved innocent. Let's go talk a little bit to Anna Julian and see what we can learn."

Together, they left the store manager's busy office and walked across the sixth floor to the quiet of the antiques concession. Cherry was just as well satisfied that Mr. Dance was nowhere around.

"He's probably upstairs consulting with the store detectives," Tom muttered. He called, "Good afternoon, Mrs. Julian. Have you a moment?"

"I'm free, as you see," Mrs. Julian said politely, coming up to them.

The woman's pallor and strained look disturbed

Cherry. Mrs. Julian must be badly shocked by the theft of the highboy, and she must realize, even if no one had told her, that this second theft could reflect on her.

"Mrs. Julian," she said in concern, "I don't at all like the way you look. I'd recommend that you go around the corner to see Dr. Murphy when you leave the store this evening, or sometime tomorrow."

"Why, you sound quite serious, Cherry!"

"I am serious. I'll write out the medical authorization form for you. Don't you agree, Tom?"

"I certainly do. Would you mind answering one more question, Mrs. Julian?" She looked weary but smiled. "Did you see the pretended agent on Friday morning?"

"I saw several people in the department on Friday morning. I'm not certain, Mr. Reese, whether I saw the man Mr. Dance described or not. Mr. Dance handled that transaction personally, you know. Mr. Dance generally does take care of the really important sales himself."

"Thank you," Tom said. "Now we won't bother you any more."

"Thank goodness! Have *you* a moment to spare? Cherry, you remember the music box I showed to you on Sunday? Here it is."

Cherry felt sorry to see the music box set out on one of the display tables. But Mrs. Julian seemed relieved to be able to talk about the music box rather than the theft, and matter of fact about parting with it. That is, if Mr. Dance were able to sell it for her, on his usual commission basis.

"Of course I'm sorry not to keep it, especially since it was a gift from my husband, but I could use the funds."

She insisted on winding the music box and playing the minuet for them. All three stood listening to the odd, plaintive melody. Mrs. Julian seemed extremely nervous today, and inclined to chatter.

"Isn't it remarkable that the first theft was of a very small object, and the second theft a very large object? Whoever is taking these things has expensive taste. I told Mr. Dance, poor man, that I've taken good care to insure my music box—"

Her chattering was not making a very good impression on Tom Reese. It was not like her, and Cherry recognized it as unease. Tom moved away, with a nod. Cherry whispered to Mrs. Julian:

"Try to relax. You mustn't worry so."

Cherry caught up with Tom in the corridor.

"Tom," Cherry pleaded, "couldn't you ask the various investigators and detectives not to be too harsh with her?"

He frowned. "They have to continue their investigations. I'll do what I can, though."

"Thank you for your kindness to Anna Julian."

"It's for you, too, Cherry," he said. "I just hope you aren't wrong about her."

His remark set Cherry to thinking back over her conversations with Mrs. Julian. With Mr. Dance, too, for that matter. What persistently came back to Cherry was Mrs. Julian's remark: "Mr. Dance doesn't know too much about antiques, he cheerfully admits it." That was plainly the reason he needed Mrs. Julian with her wide, firsthand knowledge of antiques. While she was not a scholar, like Mr. Otto, she easily outstripped Miss Janet Lamb and Adam Heller. Probably Mr. Dance could get some other knowledgeable assistant, but not as inexpensively as Mrs. Julian. No wonder he kept her on.

Yet this entire situation raised a tantalizing question. If Mr. Dance didn't know much about antiques, why was he in this business? True, he was an experienced businessman, or the store would not have given him a contract and floor space. But why was he in antiques?

Well, Cherry reasoned, there were immense sums of money to be made in the sale of, for example, the highboy. Just think of what ten or even five per cent of the sale price of the highboy would have put in Dance's pocket! Since he obtained the antiques on consignment from their owners, the emphasis was on *selling*—on the commercial aspect of the antiques business. "Then," Cherry figured, "Mr. Dance is in this business for the profits to be made, and he relies on Mrs. Julian and Mr. Otto and probably others for their specialized knowledge."

Mr. Otto . . . She walked along ruminating. "Then why," she asked herself suddenly, "was Willard Dance so agitated that time Mr. Otto called him up at the store?"

The scene flashed back into her memory—his saying, "Otto shouldn't phone me here," and the way Dance quickly covered up his agitation in front of the people in his department. The way Dance had said half-humorously, "That Otto never gives me any peace . . ." That incident was rather extraordinary. Mr. Dance had covered up so fast, she hadn't fully noticed it at the time.

But why didn't he want Otto to telephone him at the store? The store seemed the logical place to discuss antiques. Cherry recalled that Adam Heller had answered the telephone that day. Did Dance not want anyone to take Otto's messages? Otto had not left any message with old Adam Heller. What was so secret, that Dance didn't wish his assistants to know it?

Cherry could not find any answers, but a nameless, uneasy doubt about Willard Dance formed in her mind. A doubt of Otto, too? Well, she didn't know anything about Mr. Otto. It was Mr. Dance who had acted upset.

In fairness, Cherry tried to remember if being upset and excited was a regular part of Mr. Dance's temperament. No, every time she had seen him, Willard Dance had been affable and easygoing.

Another curious thing occurred to Cherry. Mr. Dance had operated his concession for many months and no thefts had ever occurred before. Now all of a sudden *two* thefts occurred, and within ten days of each other. Could Mrs. Julian be involved? But Mrs. Julian had been with the department ever since it opened, and her personal situation had been the same then as now.

Some vague uneasiness about Dance persisted. Still, Cherry had nothing tangible to go on. She wondered whether Mr. Otto, who was an experienced and established art expert, entertained any suspicions toward Willard Dance.

~~~~~~

CHAPTER VII

Strange Markings

IF THERE WERE FURTHER DEVELOPMENTS IN THE theft investigations, Cherry did not hear about them. It was maddening to work next door to the store manager's office and across the floor from the antiques department, where developments of some sort *must* be taking place—and not know about them! Cherry didn't think it a good idea, though, to bother Tom Reese any further. As for Mrs. Julian, the kindest thing one could do for her was to let her alone for a few days. Besides, Cherry found she had quite enough work to do, the balance of this first week of December, in her medical department.

She was on the train Friday morning going in to work when her attention was caught by a woman seated across the aisle. About fifty, she was a big-boned, fleshy, powerful woman in a mannish suit and unbecoming hat—big blunt features, big square hands like a butcher's. But it was what she was doing with the newspaper that puzzled Cherry. The woman was marking it with a red pencil, and she never turned the page once during the train ride.

Curious, Cherry wriggled in her seat so that she could see a little better without blatantly craning her neck. The woman was marking the page of antiques news. How could anyone stay at the same page for over half an hour?

When the train pulled into Pennsylvania Station, Cherry made it a point to stand close behind the woman with the newspaper, trying to see what the woman had underlined. Suddenly the woman turned half around, frowning down at Cherry. Cherry's heart pounded as if she had been caught eavesdropping.

"Sorry if I'm crowding you," she murmured.

The woman nodded, and Cherry was able to take a closer look at her. She had the bulging eyes and high flush of someone with a temper. She turned around and folded the marked page inside.

Then the passengers began moving onto the station platform. Cherry kept the woman in sight. Most people, having read the newspaper on the train, threw it into one of the waste bins. But this woman tucked it firmly under her arm, as if that newspaper were valuable. Cherry lost her as the crowd mounted the stairways to street level.

How strange to mark up a newspaper in that way! Was it a game? An English lesson, perhaps? Well, in a big city one found all sorts of odd people and queer things going on.

"Possibly there's some simple, reasonable explanation," Cherry thought, dismissing the incident from her mind.

That morning Cherry's first patient was an elderly man who was supervisor of the shipping department. Cherry had already looked up a health report about him, and had found something interesting. Carl Jones had a heart condition. The store had offered this long-time employee a position in some other branch of work which would be less wearing for him. Carl Jones, out of pride, had refused.

Now he walked into the medical department complaining that he felt "a little tired." Cherry knew better than to scold or question.

"Very well, Mr. Jones, perhaps you'd like to rest. There are cots in the next room."

"Well, yes, maybe that's not such a bad idea."

Cherry left the man quite alone for half an hour. Partly so that he would rest, mostly because she did not wish him to think the nurse was fussing over him. Carl Jones wanted people to think that he was an active, able man, heart condition or not.

Presently, she rapped and went in to see Mr. Jones. He swung his legs off the cot when he saw her and sat up straight.

"I'm fine again now, Nurse."

"I'm sure you are." Cherry sat down. Some patients, particularly men, and particularly older people, hated to admit any personal weakness.

"I'll just have to check your pulse, Mr. Jones." Cherry took his wrist between her thumb and forefinger, counting. Then, without letting him notice, she counted his breathing rate. Both pulse and respiration were too rapid.

"I told you I was fine," the man said defiantly.

"You pretty nearly are. What brought on the tired feeling?"—for *tired* was as much as he would admit at this point.

"Nothing, I tell you!"

"All right, if you say so."

Cherry wrote in her notebook, looking matter of fact. Her notation was unimportant but her impersonal, authoritative manner calmed Mr. Jones. She waited; the silence lengthened.

He said evasively, "I had a hard day yesterday. Didn't sleep so well last night, either."

Cherry nodded sympathetically. "I think the pressure of Christmas shoppers gets on everybody's nerves. I, for one, am looking forward to going home for Christmas."

She chatted lightly about her home in Hilton, and how living on Long Island was a nice change. That is, she completely changed the subject and Mr. Jones forgot to be on guard.

The man cleared his throat. "Ah—I suppose I was crazy to move a big packing case by myself. Oh, well —but it's not only that! Some of the extra helpers we hired temporarily—they're green kids—don't know the job. They do everything wrong! It exasperates me."

Cherry nodded and let him talk. She did *not* say he must not overexert himself nor grow exasperated. She did *not* warn, "Watch out for a heart attack, Mr. Jones." Instead, she suggested that the longest way round is the shortest way home.

"Well, Miss Ames," he said at last, "I feel a lot better. Thanks for letting me air my grievances. I guess—I guess I'd better take things a bit easier."

"It might pay off."

"You sure opened my eyes, Miss Ames."

"You opened your own eyes." This way he was really convinced, and would remain convinced, that he must face his heart condition realistically.

On Saturday morning the medical department did its usual brisk business in bruised, banged, and misplaced children. By now Cherry and Gladys took small fry and parents in stride. The youngsters always made remarkably rapid recoveries, and Cherry found that keeping a large jar of hard candies in full view was efficacious. A modest supply of toys was useful, too, except that one small girl loved the medical department's doll so much that she cried when she had to go home.

Executives did not often show up in the medical department, but on Saturday morning a man supervisor did come in, to ask Cherry to talk with a woman "who has been a frequent visitor to the clinic."

"What is her name?"

"Katie Saunders. Surely you know her. She's been in and out of here many times."

Cherry did not recall the name, nor did her assistant. She looked through the file cabinet but found no card for that name.

"Miss Ames, she says she's been here several times a week. Don't you give your patients a pass or slip or some such thing?"

"Only when it's necessary for them to leave the store or apply for a leave of absence," Cherry explained.

"Well, I'm sick and tired of having one of my crack salesclerks floating off to the medical department, while you don't even keep a record—"

"I'd like to have a talk with this Katie Saunders," said Cherry. "I'd like to study your absent-and-leaves report, too, if you don't mind."

Katie Saunders was a pretty, blond woman who

had no intention of telling the nurse anything. Cherry took a firm stand with her.

"How long have you been with Thomas and Parke, Miss Saunders?"

"Twelve years. For your information, Miss Ames, I pull down the highest commissions selling in the French Room." She gave Cherry a contemptuous look that said, "I'm an old-timer and I know all the tricks, so don't try to cross swords with me."

"Isn't it remarkable, Miss Saunders, that in twelve years there's no record of your making any visit to the medical department?"

"It's remarkable that you don't keep your records in better order!"

"That will do," Cherry retorted. She produced the supervisor's absent-and-leaves report.

"Flu. A cold. A headache," Cherry read from the supervisor's report. She studied the woman. "You look in the pink of condition to me. Look here, Miss Saunders. Either you tell me where you actually were, when you claimed to be in the medical department, or I'll send you around the corner to the doctor for a complete medical checkup."

"I won't go."

"You'll go, or you'll risk losing your job. Now the truth, please, Miss Saunders."

"You're kicking up quite a fuss about this two-by-four first-aid corner, aren't you?" the woman snapped.

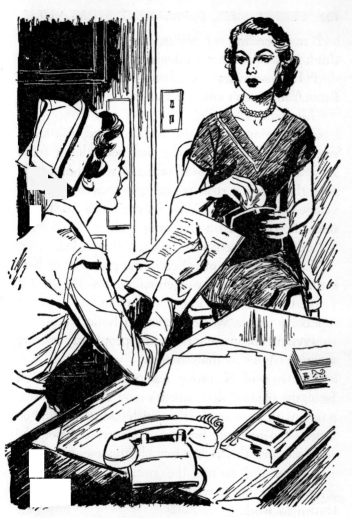

"Now the truth, please, Miss Saunders,"
Cherry said firmly

"I'm defending my professional reputation. Don't think it's simply your word against mine, Miss Saunders! I have written records and can back up what I say. You haven't any proof at all."

"All right, all right!"

Coolly, almost as if she were amused, the saleswoman recounted what she had been doing for a long while now. She was perfectly well, but whenever there was a rush period, she conveniently developed a "headache." When there was a too-strenuous sale, she faked a coughing spell.

"And where were you?" Cherry demanded.

"Enjoying a cup of coffee in the cafeteria, or having a cigarette in the women employees' lounge. Or I could always duck into a washroom."

Cherry sent a written report to Katie Saunders's supervisor. Fortunately not many people in the store were as odious as that woman.

The rest of Saturday was pleasanter. Though busy, the medical department's most serious case was a man with a sprained wrist which had to be plunged repeatedly into very hot water. Cherry did not like to administer this uncomfortable treatment, but the hot water did reduce the swelling at once. She strapped the man's wrist firmly, and he was able to return to work.

As Cherry expected, the balance of Saturday was filled mostly with small fry. Quite a number of sales-

clerks, too, reported to the store hospital with headaches, backaches, and just plain "nerves."

"I suppose we can expect an increasing number
of 'casualties' the nearer we come to Christmas,"
Cherry remarked to her assistant during Saturday's
one lull.

Cherry had already worked out split-shift schedules for Gladys and herself, since the store was now
open from nine A.M. to nine P.M. They took turns
with the two shifts, which were nine A.M. to five
P.M., and two P.M. to nine P.M. Sometimes Cherry
came in to work at eight A.M., to put the clinic in
readiness, and left at four P.M.

"But no one ever told me," Cherry said plaintively,
"that the peak periods would be as hectic as this."

"Me, either," said Gladys. "This is the first time
I've sat down for more than two minutes today!"

Cherry was thinking that at last she would have a
chance to wash her face when a messenger brought a
report from Dr. Murphy. The report dealt with Mrs.
Julian.

"Mrs. Anna Julian, complete checkup, 12/4.
Blood count, normal. A slight secondary anemia for
which vitamins are prescribed. Physically and or-
ganically sound. Dental report satisfactory. Patient's
accelerated pulse and feelings of exhaustion apparently caused by anxiety, since no physical symptoms
are present."

Cherry read the doctor's report twice, to make sure she understood correctly. It was plain that Mrs. Julian's worried state of mind was indirectly hurting her health. The doctor's report underlined the urgency of clearing up the two thefts and exonerating Mrs. Julian. The mental strain was making her ill.

"If Anna Julian reacts so sharply in two weeks," Cherry thought, "imagine if the questioning drags on for months! She might break down altogether. No, something has to be done, and promptly."

But what was to be done? All she had to go on so far were some half-defined doubts about Dance.

When Cherry left the department store late that afternoon, she joined the crowd and walked through the colorful main floor. Crystal snowflakes and bisque angels floated above aisles thronged with shoppers. People jostled along slowly, good-humored.

Suddenly Cherry noticed just ahead of her a stout, mannish woman who looked vaguely familiar. Yes, she was the woman who'd marked the newspaper so oddly on the train yesterday morning. Today, again, she clutched a folded newspaper tightly under her arm, and she was hurrying, elbowing people aside. Cherry kept her eye on the woman's felt hat and tried to keep pace with her. But it was hopeless.

"Oh, well, what am I chasing her for, anyway? What of it, if she marked up a newspaper?"

Purely out of curiosity, when Cherry reached

Pennsylvania Station and boarded her waiting train, she walked through all the cars, looking at the passengers. The woman was nowhere to be seen.

"Maybe she doesn't keep regular hours, like other commuters," Cherry decided as she sank into the next vacant seat she came to. "Still, she wouldn't have been on an early-morning train unless she had some business in town. Women shoppers don't come in quite that early. Wonder what she does?" On Monday morning's train, she would look for the woman again.

Then she settled down more comfortably into the seat and let the rocking speed of the train soothe her. Thank goodness for week ends!

"And when I was a student at Spencer, I thought nursing was romantic!"

~~~~~~

CHAPTER VIII

Errand Or Excuse?

MONDAY MORNING ON THE TRAIN CHERRY MADE a point of walking through the cars but she did not see the stout woman again. On Tuesday, although her interest was waning, Cherry looked again. All she got for her trouble was a cramped seat in a corner of the smoking car, the only seat left by the time she had scanned the passengers. Well, she had tried and satisfied her curiosity. Now she might as well forget about the ungainly woman and her newspaper.

Besides, this morning, Cherry had something more interesting to think about. The antiques department was holding a special art exhibit today and three or four art experts and collectors were coming to the department to speak, at Mr. Dance's invitation. Cherry had already seen the announcement in Sunday's paper and in this morning's paper. One of the speakers was to be Mr. Elbert Otto.

By two o'clock such a large number of visitors had congregated across the floor from the medical department that Gladys said, "What's happening over there in antiques? You'd think a movie star was coming, or something."

Even from here Cherry could see extra display cases and tables, spread with all sorts of Georgian silver and Sheffield plate, with Lowestoft porcelain and Royal Worcester china services. Against one wall Mr. Dance was still arranging, of all things, a collection of cigar-store Indians and other American trade signs of an earlier time. They looked incongruously out of place alongside French furniture and shelves of first-edition books. No doubt extra store detectives were on duty.

"I'd like to take twenty or thirty minutes off," Cherry said, "and listen to what Mr. Otto has to say. I could do desk work half an hour longer, to catch up."

"Go ahead," her assistant urged. "I'll hold the fort. If anything urgent comes up, I'll come and get you."

"We'll see how our work goes."

By two thirty nothing much was happening in the medical department. By three, when Mr. Otto ponderously stood up to speak, Cherry slipped across the corridor. She sat down on one of the folding chairs at the rear of the audience. These men and women —mostly men and probably art specialists—were absorbedly interested. They exchanged remarks among themselves; many seemed to know one another. They awarded Mr. Otto a spattering of applause as Willard Dance introduced him. As usual, Otto carried his large official-looking brief case, bulging from long use, and set it on the speaker's table.

"He looks like a bull," Cherry thought, as Otto stood before the table which held Oriental porcelains, his specialty apparently, or one of his specialties. "A lumbering bull who'd trample anything out of his path."

He took the first plate in his thick hands and held it up to show the audience. Even though Otto spoke with a surprisingly delicate appreciation, Cherry still could not like the man. The arrogance of his stare and stance—the way he coldly flattered his audience —the heavy voice—no, she had never seen anyone so ugly.

"Now, gentlemen—your pardon, *ladies* and gentlemen—you have heard me on other occasions praise Willard Dance's collection. In all my experience I have not seen better or more complete. Look, if you please, at the unusual colorings on this Lowestoft—"

Otto's remarks became technical and Cherry's attention wandered. She saw Mr. Dance sitting modestly at one side of the speaker, smiling. He nodded and waved to some people tiptoeing in. How could that man be so unruffled, considering the highboy

theft and the immense claim against him by its owner's insurance company? Cherry could not understand
it, unless Dance were an awfully good actor.

"Though of course he can't go around advertising
his worry, I suppose. Perhaps," she thought, "today's
exhibit is his effort to drum up extra business, and
earn his way out of that staggering debt."

So far she had not spotted Mrs. Julian and now
Cherry saw her. Mrs. Julian whispered to Dance, who
handed her a key. She opened a glass case, and removed her music box which she set within Otto's
reach. Anna Julian was smiling but pale. Then she
returned the key to Mr. Dance, and sat down across
the room from Cherry.

"Now this delightful music box," said Otto, reaching for it. "Here we have a rarity. I would fix its date
at circa 1790, and you will note"—he held up the
hand-painted wooden box "—its maker's name is en-
graved on the small metal plate at the back. You see?
Yes, Munich, 1794, what did I say?"

He inclined his bulletshaped head and wound
the handle. Cherry stole a look at Mrs. Julian. She
seemed quite pleased at the attention Mr. Otto was
giving to her music box, a compliment to her taste.
And probably, Cherry thought, this would help to
sell it. After the audience had listened to the tinkling
minuet, the music box was handed around for the
visitors and other experts to examine.

"Hist!" It was Gladys Green tapping Cherry's shoulder. "You're wanted on the telephone, Miss Ames. Routine call from Dr. Murphy's office nurse, but you'd better come."

"Thanks, Gladys. I've spent twenty minutes here anyway, that's enough."

As Cherry left, she heard Mr. Dance announcing:

"I'm sure you'd all like to know that my assistant, Mrs. Julian, will soon be doing something new and interesting—"

Cherry turned, rather startled. Was Mrs. Julian changing jobs? Was she leaving Thomas and Parke?

"—new for her, I mean to say," Mr. Dance went on. "Of course I've had occasion to tell many of you how very gifted this lady is, how very knowledgeable about *objets d'art*—"

He was so long-winded! Cherry lingered as long as she dared, but had to return to her duties.

There was no chance to stop by at the antiques department again, but Mrs. Julian herself came into the store hospital Wednesday morning with some proud news. Having a few free minutes, Cherry led her into the adjoining room with the cots. Mrs. Julian was too excited to sit down.

"To tell you the truth, Cherry, I'm quite surprised. I'm still not used to such an important assignment!"

"But what *is* it?"

"Mr. Dance is sending me on a buying trip, if you please. He's entrusting me with purchases for his collection! Oh, it's just to New England. A short trip, up to Portland, then back to Boston, which is an antiques center. I'll be back by Christmas or a few days later. But isn't it encouraging?"

"I'm so glad for you." Cherry had not expected Mrs. Julian would be leaving town. "Yes, it certainly is encouraging. It's your first buying trip?"

"Yes. Mr. Dance says I've proved my ability. Besides, Cherry, I think he's sending me in order to show his confidence in me—as a kind of retort to those detectives. Mr. Dance as much as said so, in that tactful way of his."

"Well, it will be a nice change for you," Cherry said guardedly.

Anna Julian sighed. "I'm glad to go—so glad to get away from the suspicion in the store for a little while."

"Of course you will be coming back, won't you?"

"Why, Cherry, what a question! Certainly. I shall resume my job after this trip." Uneasiness crept into Mrs. Julian's face. "Why? Do you feel there's anything unusual about my being sent on this trip?"

Cherry hesitated. "Oh, no—no, I think it's fine. It's just a surprise, that's all." She could scarcely say to Mrs. Julian that Mr. Dance's decision to send her away was unexpected and that she'd like to know all of Dance's reasons. "I—I suppose you've bought for Mr. Dance before?"

"Well, no, this is the first time. That's why it's a proof of his confidence in me. Particularly at a time when there's so much difficulty in our department."

A pointed time to get Anna Julian off the scene, Cherry thought, but she said tactfully, "Yes, it is a difficult time for Mr. Dance."

"Poor man! Do you know, he's been defending me all along to the store detectives?"

He *said* he had, Cherry amended silently. If he had, why did the unrelenting questioning of Mrs. Julian continue?

"And now he's entrusting me to act as his representative, to buy a melodeon and a cradle." Mrs. Julian smiled and shook her head. "It's quite a pat on the back. If you knew how that man loves his business! He feels he has to do everything himself. Janet Lamb or Adam Heller or I couldn't do things *perfectly* enough to suit him! Why, he carries the keys to the display cases in his pocket and we have to ask him for a key every time we wish to show a locked-up article to a customer. Ever since the jade vase was stolen, he guards those keys like a jealous lover, and sometimes he locks some of the things away in closets. Mr. Dance says we shouldn't have *every* item out on display all the time, too boring. He believes it intrigues customers to come in and discover that lovely yellow lamp they had their eye on is no longer on display. Then the customer gets panicky, thinking someone else has bought it, and when Mr. Dance produces it from the closet, usually the customer snaps it up." Mrs. Julian giggled. "The way Mr. Dance does things! As if his business were his favorite game."

"Yes, some business heads do insist on using their own personal systems. Or taking direct charge of everything themselves," Cherry murmured. But she remembered how Dance had not wanted his staff to take Otto's telephone messages, either, how upset Dance had been.

"All the same," Cherry ventured, "and though I recognize antiques is an unusual business with rules of its own, I can't help wondering."

It puzzled her, Cherry said, that although Mr. Dance had supplied a most detailed description of the "agent" who "bought" the highboy from him, the detectives had not turned up the slightest clue or lead to the swindler. This, in spite of the fact that three sets of detectives—store, city, and insurance company—were working on the case.

"Surely you don't mean to suggest, Cherry, that the thefts were staged from inside our department?"

"Surely *something*, some lead, would have turned up? The detectives haven't the faintest clue about who took the Ming vase, either."

"It's been only two or three weeks—"

Mrs. Julian looked so bewildered that Cherry forbore to say the rest of what was on her mind. How much did Mr. Dance really know about these thefts? Why was he so untroubled and philosophical about them, considering that he would have to make repayment in full for the highboy?

"I just wish I knew more facts about—oh, everything," Cherry said thoughtfully. "You've known Mr. Dance for some time, haven't you? And so has Mr. Otto, I suppose?"

"Yes, Mr. Otto has been his consultant for quite a time. Elbert Otto is a thorough art scholar and an old hand in the field. Don't you think their working together speaks well for Mr. Dance?"

"Yes, it does. I suppose Mr. Otto has talked to you sometimes about Willard Dance?" But Mrs. Julian did not know Otto very well. Cherry had an idea. "Mrs. Julian, you said just now that Boston is an antiques center. Is there an antiques dealers' association in Boston?"

"Yes, the main headquarters is in Boston."

"Well, would you think me very inquisitive if I asked you to make a routine business inquiry about Mr. Dance at the association? About his standing and his past activity. Just for curiosity's sake?"

Anna Julian seemed amused but she said, "If you wish. An inquiry can't do any harm." Then her face grew serious; she finally gathered that Cherry was trying to hint at something.

"I don't mean to sound unreasonable about your Mr. Dance. I expect I'm mistaken—just a random thought."

"I know how it is, one does get disturbing impressions about people." Mrs. Julian confided in a rush, "I'm ashamed of myself, but I don't much care for Mr. Otto. Not for any reason I can name. *He* vaguely troubles me, though it's nothing more than my unreasonable aversion to the man."

"Why don't you inquire about Mr. Otto, too, as long as you're in Boston?" Cherry suggested.

"Perhaps I shall. I *am* grateful to Mr. Otto for featuring my music box yesterday afternoon. Mr. Dance says any number of people were intrigued, and that he promptly put it out of sight in the closet." Mrs. Julian chuckled. "His private system. It does stimulate sales."

"Music boxes and melodeons." Cherry smiled. "You seem to be in charge of music for your department."

"Of course," Mrs. Julian said with a laugh, "Mr. Dance isn't asking me to buy anything as valuable as the highboy or the rose diamond necklace. But still!"

"I hope you have a good trip. Really good."

"Thank you, Cherry. I must go now, because I leave this afternoon."

They exchanged good-bys. Mrs. Julian was halfway across the corridor when Cherry suddenly remembered a question she wanted to ask. She ran after her friend.

"It's an awfully random question, I'm afraid, but since we've aired everything else that's on our minds— Do you happen to know an ungainly stout woman, who wears very strictly tailored things, about fifty years old?" She checked herself from adding, "The woman was marking the antiques page."

But Mrs. Julian did not know such a woman, even though Cherry filled in descriptive details.

Cherry returned to the medical department, feeling rather foolish. She hoped that Mrs. Julian's assignment was not a contrived errand. If it were, that would demoralize Mrs. Julian still more. Did Mr. Dance genuinely want her to buy for him? Or, if he desired to remove Mrs. Julian from his department for a while, the price of a melodeon and a cradle was cheap enough as an excuse. Errand or excuse? Cherry wondered.

That evening, although she was having a date with Tom Reese, the topic of conversation was still Mrs. Julian. Cherry liked the restaurant where she and Tom were dining, she liked being dressed up in a black dress and gay cap, and she liked having Tom Reese across the table from her. She would gladly have talked to him of other, lighter things, but Tom was surprised when she mentioned Mrs. Julian's trip. As surprised as she herself had been.

"Dance didn't advise our office about any buying trip for Anna Julian," Tom said. "Perhaps he notified Personnel. When is she leaving, Cherry?"

"She left this afternoon."

Tom let out a low whistle. "Dance sent her away on short notice. Almost in a hurry."

"Mmmm. That's what I thought, too." She scanned his smooth face; his dark eyes studied his plate, then lifted to hers.

"What do you make of this trip, Cherry? Think Dance is on the level in sending her?" Then, all at once, Tom smiled because they so often thought alike. "All right, I know we agree. But what did Dance send her away for?"

"We-ll. Advice, please, boss."

He said quickly, "I'm not your boss. Certainly not after hours. What advice?"

"Could Willard Dance do anything special in Mrs. Julian's absence—anything he can't do while she's around? Such as"—Cherry swallowed hard—"prosecuting her?"

Tom nodded. "That occurs to me, too. To prosecute is fairly drastic. Besides, I doubt that he has any complete proof against her. Let's hope not! But what he could do is say a lot of snide things against her to the detectives."

"Sort of prove her guilty of theft, behind her back?"

"Could be. Perhaps he hasn't quite the nerve to accuse her while she's around." Tom frowned, endeavoring to be fair. "Dance may be convinced she's a thief. And I don't think he sent her all that distance to look at an insignificant melodeon and cradle. Wouldn't justify the expenses of her trip."

When Tom, who usually was gay and smiling grew so serious, something was wrong. Cherry asked him about the store's attitude, and he gave her a direct answer. As a store executive, he knew fully the gravity of what Anna Julian would have to face. He described, rather grimly, store methods of dealing with suspect employees, and of possible penalties to Mrs. Julian.

"For example," Tom said, "she'd not only lose her job at Thomas and Parke, but she'd be blacklisted with every store in town, for future employment. Eventually the word would get around to stores and galleries in other cities, as well."

"Tom, that won't really come to pass, will it?"

"We'll do our best not to let it happen."

She told him that, at her request, Mrs. Julian planned while in Boston to check with the antiques dealers' association headquarters on Dance and possibly Otto. Tom was reassured to hear that.

For a while they talked around and around the

matter of the two thefts, trying on their ideas for size, Tom said. Cherry wondered about whether Dance himself might have played a part in the disappearance of the highboy. Tom half agreed her idea might not be farfetched. No one but Dance, he pointed out, had seen or talked to the so-called agent. Dance's story on the highboy was the sole information they had. Encouraged, she ventured that *maybe*, only maybe, Dance himself might have been involved in the theft of the tiny Ming vase. But Tom would not go out on a limb for that hypothesis, lacking any facts to go on.

"We need facts," he said over coffee. "Say, what kind of a date is this? Who are we?"

"Reese and Ames, confidential agents. Bring us your problems."

"Our problem, young lady, is where shall we go next? Too early for dancing. Drive? A movie? No! I can't talk to you in a movie."

They settled for a drive, rolling along the speedways which circled Manhattan Island. At the right side of them rose the lighted, towering city; on their left flowed the night-black East River, alive with lighted ships and spanned with long, lighted bridges.

"It's a fairyland of lights," Cherry said, enjoying herself. "You'd think it was a giant carnival."

"Isn't New York fabulous? See how pale the stars look in comparison. Are you warm enough?"

Tom swung the car around the tip of the island near Wall Street, and they drove uptown along the broad Hudson River with the immense city buildings rising like cliffs above the river. As they drove, they talked, and Tom told Cherry something about himself. He came from Pennsylvania, where his parents still lived, in a lovely mountain town; he'd attended the University of Pennsylvania, served a hitch in the army, and found his first job at Thomas and Parke.

"I liked it so well I just stayed."

"The store apparently likes you, too. Didn't they promote you awfully fast?"

"I *earned* my promotions. I've worked harder in New York than anywhere else in my life. Everybody does here. It's the terrific competition, the New York pace. I love it. Work hard, play hard. Speaking of play—"

It was ten o'clock, and Tom declared it was time they went somewhere to dance. He had a favorite place he'd discovered, not yet famous and crowded, and he wanted Cherry to know he didn't tell everybody about it—"only my favorite people."

It was just a small place, with photographs of musicians on the walls, and a dance floor approximately the size of a postage stamp. Only two couples bothered to dance; everyone else sat listening intently to the music of the jazz quintet. Cherry found the coffee here another pleasant surprise. They served twenty different kinds of coffee, from all the countries of the world. Cherry chose Viennese coffee, a big creamy cupful heaped with whipped cream. Tom enjoyed a demitasse of black pungent Italian *expresso*, served with a bit of lemon peel.

"Sometime," Tom promised, "we'll come here and go straight through the coffee list. We'll try all twenty kinds, between us."

"If we drink that much coffee all in one evening, we won't be able to sleep for a week!"

"Right, Nurse. I forgot. Want to dance?"

They danced well together. They returned to their table for more coffee, more music, and completely lost track of the time. Only when the musicians left their instruments and walked off for a break did Tom remember to look at his wrist watch.

"Guess what time?" Tom asked.

"Eleven. Or a little bit more."

"It's midnight. Not that I care. I can stay up all night and feel fine tomorrow."

"Well, I can't," Cherry said. "And tomorrow is a working day."

"Spoken like a true New Yorker. Waiter! Check, and the pumpkin chariot."

Outside, Tom urged her to try "just one more little place, for ham and eggs," but Cherry knew her eyes were heavy and her nose must be shiny.

"Cinderella has to go home now," she said. "Thanks all the same, Prince."

"Where did we park the pumpkin chariot? Oh, my gosh, I can't remember where I parked the car!"

Up one street and down another they wandered. Tom called under his breath, "Here, Chrysler! Come on out, nice old Chrysler! Hey, W843, answer your master!"

Cherry was convulsed with laughter. They finally located his car on East Fifty-fifth Street. "I do this all the time," Tom admitted.

"You ought to train your boy to sound his horn when you call him."

"All right, Cherry, all right. I know it's *me* who's lost. Where to?"

For tonight, Cherry was staying over at No. 9. Tom drove her down to the Village in ten minutes and saw her safely inside the door.

"Tom, it's been a delightful evening. Thank you so much."

"Thank *you* for the date, Cherry. Let's do it again soon—if I don't mislay the car."

"Now good night, unless we should say good morning."

"That's right! See you first thing tomorrow morning on the elevator. Three cheers for Thomas and Parke!"

CHAPTER IX

Private Gallery

"NIGHT LIFE ISN'T FOR ME," CHERRY SAID, YAWN-ing. Bertha, squeezed in the kitchenette, handed her a glass of orange juice bright and early Thursday morning. "I feel as if I'd been asleep only two minutes."

"I hated to wake you," Vivian said sympathetically. "Here, you carry the tray of coffee things and I'll take the rolls and plates."

Bertha followed them. Then little Mai Lee and tall Betty Lane came staggering sleepily into No. 9's small dining room. "Slug-a-beds," Bertha said. "You should try living on a farm like my family's, and wake up with the chickens."

"The chickens would never see me," Betty promised. She collapsed onto a chair. "How was the date, Cherry?"

Cherry was obliged to recount every detail, but she would not divulge the address of Tom's pet place.

"You're a meanie," said Mai Lee. "You know how I love small jazz units."

"Honestly it isn't my place to tell about," Cherry said. "But I'll ask Tom for permission to tell you. The fascinating places there are in New York!"

"That place sounds dreamy," Betty said. As nurse-companion to an elderly woman, she was fairly confined. "Wouldn't you love to know about all the places in this town? The other day my employer, Mrs. McIntosh, received an invitation in the mail to visit a private art and antiques gallery, in a Long Island mansion, if you please."

"A what?" Cherry asked sharply. "What was the name of the place or the owner?"

"I think it was called Otto Galleries."

"Cherry," Bertha objected, "you're not eating a thing."

"Sorry, Bertha darling, I will—in a minute— Betty, do you think I might see that invitation?"

"Oh, I'm afraid Mrs. McIntosh threw it away several days ago. You know, she's interested in antiques. But, poor lady, she doesn't often feel well enough to leave her apart— Why, Cherry, what are you so excited about?"

"Betty, try to remember!" Cherry urged her. "What did the invitation say?"

Betty and the other girls were staring at her. Betty answered:

"It was a printed invitation, but it seems to me the envelope was handwritten. Mrs. McIntosh is on so many mailing lists I don't quite— Anyway, it was apparently one of those invitations that's sent to selected lists of persons. And it said you could see this collection of antiques in the collector's home. By appointment."

"It wasn't a museum, was it?" Cherry frowned. "The art and antiques were for sale?"

"Well, Mrs. McIntosh said, 'I'm not going to buy another thing,' and threw the invitation away."

"Just one more question. *Where* on Long Island was the private gallery?"

Betty Lane shrugged. "I don't remember—yes, perhaps I do. There was the name *Woodacres* on the invitation. But whether that's the name of the house or an estate or even a village somewhere on Long Island—"

"Thank you very much indeed!" To the other girls, Cherry promised to tell them the whole story some day. That is, if she ever found out all there was to know.

She rushed off to work, thinking how valuable this piece of news about the Otto Galleries might turn out to be. A real and important find! Mr. Otto might certainly be running a bona fide gallery and business.

Or he might be a receiver, an outlet for stolen goods. Sending invitations to a select list of patrons was a recognized method used by all art dealers. Still, Cherry reflected, it would give a not-too-honest dealer a chance to screen his potential customers. He could easily keep out anyone he wished. Also, housing the art objects and antiques in a private house would give Otto a chance to keep secret whatever he had for sale—if secrecy were advisable.

But by the time she approached the store, Cherry had some second thoughts. In the first place, what if there were a connection between Elbert Otto and Otto Galleries? She happened to know of Mr. Otto as an art consultant, but there was no reason why he should not also run his own gallery, perhaps as a secondary business. The fact that he operated it in a private house, possibly his home—well, how usual or unusual was that?

At the sixth floor, Cherry stopped first in the antiques department. Miss Janet Lamb was already there, her gray head bent as she lovingly dusted a Chinese figurine of rose quartz. They said good-mornings, hoped Mrs. Julian was having good weather in Portland, and then Cherry asked:

"Would you clear up a question for me, please? I'd like to know whether dealers in arts and antiques often have their galleries in private houses? Or in their homes?"

Miss Janet Lamb smiled gently. "My dear child, so much depends on what the dealer can afford. In many New York galleries, the dealer has his own apartment in back of the exhibition rooms. Or sometimes he maintains a large, even elaborate household upstairs, over the gallery. Or, if he wishes, he may live elsewhere, and maintain two addresses, one for business, one for residence."

"I see." Cherry had been about to ask whether she knew the Otto Galleries, but whether Miss Lamb did or didn't, she might mention to Mr. Dance that Miss Ames had queried her. Cherry did not want any complications, certainly not any she could prevent.

"Well—ah—Miss Lamb, are you familiar with any art or antiques galleries on Long Island?"

"There's the Old Barn, and Mrs. Polly Matthew's Antiques Fair, and dozens of smaller places. You know, my dear, everyone with her grandmother's old claptrap to sell fancies she's in the antiques business."

Cherry laughed. "I'll be careful not to buy any old buggy whips. Thank you very much, Miss Lamb."

Cherry moved into the corridor, thinking that Miss Lamb had not mentioned the Otto Galleries. Why not? Was it a secret, or rather, with its selected list of clients, had it not come to Miss Lamb's attention? Or, more likely, was it something recent and not yet generally known? It occurred to Cherry that Mrs. Julian had never mentioned the Otto Galleries to her, not even when they discussed Mr. Otto yesterday. True, Mrs. Julian had made it clear that she had only a slight acquaintance with the formidable Otto. Still, it was odd.

As she did routine desk work, another part of Cherry's mind was busy with tantalizing questions. There were no patients yet; Gladys Green would not report in today until two P.M., the late shift. So Cherry had a little time and quiet in which to reflect.

First question. Were the Otto Galleries owned by Elbert Otto? Probably, since Otto as a last name was not common. Cherry got out the Manhattan telephone directory, but no Elbert Otto was listed. Then she borrowed the Long Island directory from the personnel department, and looked up Otto. Yes, there was the listing:

Otto, Elbert—
   Woodacres, North Rd. . . . CRanston 5–4122

The telephone exchange name—wasn't there a village called Cranston on Long Island? Cherry did not know where North Road was, but Aunt Kathy might.

Having the name and address did not answer her big questions. Even if she visited Woodacres, she would want to have some advance information about what she was walking into. Cherry wished Mrs. Julian weren't in Portland, but in Boston where she could check with the headquarters of the antiques dealers' association.

"But I can check, myself! There must be a branch of the dealers' association here in New York City."

Cherry was not certain of the association's name, and asking that question in the antiques department might arouse suspicion. She consulted the Manhattan telephone book, and at last found the number she wanted. Cherry wrote it down and tucked the note carefully in her purse.

When her assistant came on duty at two P.M., after an uneventful morning in the medical department, Cherry left on her lunch hour. Her first stop was a telephone booth. She dialed the dealers' association number. A man's voice answered, a pleasant voice.

"I wonder if you can tell me, please," Cherry said, "where I can locate Elbert Otto?"

"Otto? Is he a member of the association?"

"I'm not sure," said Cherry. "I know he is an art and antiques consultant and works with dealers, but whether he *is* a dealer—?"

"Just a moment, I'll look it up." A pause, then the man's voice came on again. "Yes, we do have an Elbert Otto as a member. We have two addresses for him. Do you want to write them down?"

Two addresses! This was news!

"I'm ready," said Cherry. "Please go ahead."

"Our records show Otto Galleries listed at 625 Madison Avenue—I beg your pardon, this commercial address was given up just a short time ago. We have a home address for Mr. Otto—it's Woodacres, North Road, Cranston, Long Island. Presumably Mr. Otto operates his gallery in his home now," said the man, "that is, if he operates it at all."

"Thank you very much for your advice," Cherry said, and hung up.

Why had Otto given up his city gallery? Unable to afford two rentals? But between the two locations, why had he chosen the less accessible Long Island address? It was his home address. Cherry recalled Miss Lamb's saying that sometimes dealers combined galleries and apartment, or sometimes they needed separate living quarters. Cherry considered dashing up to 625 Madison Avenue on her lunch hour, to try to learn whether that building was entirely commercial or whether it housed living quarters, too. But she would never make it, there and back, on her lunch hour.

"Anyhow, now that Mr. Otto is no longer at that address, it probably would be wasted effort for me to go up there. The *real* question is: Did Otto move his gallery to his house for a business or economy reason—or for some other reason?"

The thing to do was to go to Woodacres and find out.

Cherry's first impulse was to rush to Woodacres and improvise her way once she got there. But Aunt Kathy and Gwen, who knew about the thefts and Mrs. Julian's predicament, insisted on talking things over first, before attempting to get into Woodacres.

"You've said yourself, Cherry," Aunt Kathy reminded her at home that same evening, "that Dance, or Otto—or both!—*might* not be honest men. *If* Otto is up to something questionable, an uninvited guest might not be welcome. Particularly you, Cherry. You might be conceivably putting yourself in danger if you go to Woodacres."

Gwen laughed, then quickly apologized. "Forgive me, Aunt Kathy. But telling Cherry Ames that a place or person is dangerous—well, you're wasting your breath."

Cherry made a face at Gwen and turned to the older woman. "There's a lot of truth in what you say, Aunt Kathy. I don't want to walk in blindly. I know it's asking for trouble to enter houses or buildings one knows nothing about. Very well, then, let's see what we can learn about Woodacres."

"I was hoping," Aunt Kathy said, "that you'd drop the idea of going there at all."

"I can't. Don't you see? If I'm ever to help Mrs. Julian—" Cherry again explained her reasons.

Gwen refused to take Cherry seriously. She called her "Miss Sleuth," and declared Otto was probably selling rare old hooked rugs made last week in a factory in Trenton, New Jersey.

"Very funny," said Cherry, after Gwen had joshed her all the following evening, too.

"Stop teasing her, Gwen," said Aunt Kathy. "Even though I wish Cherry would forget the whole matter, I can see it means a lot to her. It could be an awfully serious thing for Mrs. Julian."

Gwen hooted. "Why, Aunt Kathy! I think you're becoming intrigued yourself."

Her aunt suggested they change the subject.

Saturday evening was unseasonably balmy. The three of them were just coming out of a restaurant, after dinner, and felt pleasantly lazy. They walked over to Gwen's parked car.

"Look at the moon rising over the trees," said Gwen. "Let's go for a drive. Who wants to be chauffeur?"

"I'll drive," said Aunt Kathy. "It's safer that way. No criticism intended, of course."

Sitting three abreast, with Gwen in the middle and Cherry beside the window, they rode along through the suburban town, then out onto the highway.

"Let's get off onto a quieter road," Aunt Kathy said at the wheel.

"What about North Road?" Cherry asked. "Is it quiet?"

Neither Gwen nor her aunt remembered North Road very well.

"Woodacres is located there," Cherry reminded them. "It's near the village of Cranston."

She reached into the glove compartment, took out the road map, and consulted it by flashlight.

"Sleuthing again," Gwen teased her.

"We can turn off just up ahead," Aunt Kathy said. "Which way to Cranston?"

It lay farther out on Long Island than their own village, and was another pretty cluster of suburban homes, schools, and shops. After passing through the village of Cranston, they found themselves driving along shadowy North Road. Houses were few and far between along here.

"Please, could you go a little more slowly?" Cherry asked. "I don't know whether Woodacres is a house or an estate or a section."

Aunt Kathy obligingly slowed the car. No sign reading Woodacres came into view, but the sight of the moon and the stars shining above the country road was lovely. Gradually the trees on either side of the road grew more numerous; not another car passed them in this heavily wooded area. Cherry felt a tingle of excitement.

"Let's see if we can catch a glimpse of a house," she

said. "A large house, I'd suppose, from its name. Look, there's a stone fence along here! Maybe it belongs to a house."

Now the car was moving at a crawl. The only sound in the silence was the engine's purr. Cherry strained forward, peering from one side of the road to the other. Gwen muttered, "It certainly is quiet and lonesome way out here."

"Look!" Cherry cried softly. "Do you see lights way back among the trees?"

The road was so dark here, the moonlight so filtered and lost in the woods, that it was hard to see. To help, Aunt Kathy dimmed the headlights as low as possible. She stopped the car, engine idling.

"Way back among the trees," Cherry insisted.

Aunt Kathy said suddenly, "Yes, I see them."

"Those are car lights on another road," said Gwen.

"They're not moving and you don't hear anything, do you?" Cherry countered. "No, it's a house, all right."

"A sizable house, I'd say," murmured Aunt Kathy.

The house was set far back from the road. It was, moreover, the only house around here. Cherry felt intensely curious. Was this Woodacres? A driveway led into the grounds, but she could not make out any sign, nor any placard with a place name.

"Well?" Gwen demanded. "What do we do next?"

"We might continue driving up North Road,"

Cherry said, "and see whether there are any other houses. Or any place called Woodacres."

Aunt Kathy agreed. "Wouldn't you like to drive, Cherry?"

As Cherry got out to exchange places, she heard over the engine's purr the first extraneous sound on this road for ten or fifteen minutes. Someone was whistling, in snatches. A man whistling, she'd guess. He seemed to be on this road, walking somewhere in the stillness and dark. Not very near them—the whistling held her transfixed, although she could not imagine why.

"Cherry?" Gwen prodded her. "What is it?"

"Nothing—just someone whistling. Would you mind waiting a minute?"

Cherry could not identify the tune, but it rang a bell in her memory. Could it be one of the songs the quintet had played at Tom's place? She had heard so much music the other evening with Tom that all the melodies ran together and blurred in her memory.

"Cherry?" This time it was Aunt Kathy. "Is anything wrong? I'm all gooseflesh."

"Nothing wrong. I'm coming right away."

Cherry peered one last time into the shadows ahead. She could not see anyone. The whistling was moving farther away. Then it stopped and all again was silence.

"See if you notice anyone on the road," Cherry asked her two companions, as she slid into the driver's seat.

The whistling held her transfixed,

Very slowly they drove farther up North Road. Not a soul was to be seen, although moonlight dappled the shadows here and there. Nor was there any

although she could not imagine why

other house. Farther up the road, the woods thinned out. Houses appeared, in increasing numbers. Then, abruptly, North Road led into a brightly lighted traffic circle. Cherry tried driving beyond the circle but North Road had run its course.

"Well, apparently that house back there was Woodacres," she said.

"Are you satisfied now, Miss Sleuth?" Gwen teased.

They joked about their expedition into the dark, but Cherry thought the jokes sounded forced. As for herself, the whistler's notes repeated themselves insistently in her mind. Unluckily the whole tune refused to come back to her. Cherry concentrated so much on recapturing the melody that Aunt Kathy had to say, "Watch where you're driving, dear."

"What are you humming?" Gwen asked.

"I? I didn't know I *was* humming." If the man had only whistled the tune clear through, she wouldn't have this maddening recollection of only wisps of it. "Gwen? Aunt Kathy? Can you recall the tune that man was whistling?"

Gwen hadn't paid attention to the whistler. Aunt Kathy had, and whistled for Cherry what she thought she had heard.

"Or am I confusing it with that new waltz that's so popular?"

"I guess I'm the one who's confused," Cherry said.

On reaching home, they found it was nearly eleven o'clock. All three of them were sleepy.

Half an hour later Cherry tucked herself in, but sleep had fled. The broken tune was playing over and over in her mind like a cracked phonograph record.

"Perhaps if I whistle it aloud, the complete melody will come back to me. A waltz, Aunt Kathy said."

She whistled softly, and to her astonishment the notes shifted of their own accord from a waltz rhythm into another rhythm, slower, more measured—why, it was a minuet!

Shaken, Cherry switched on the bedside lamp and sat up. The melody was the minuet of Mrs. Julian's music box! That was what the man on North Road had been whistling! It could not be mere coincidence that someone near Otto Galleries was whistling that tune. What did it mean?

"It could mean a great deal," Cherry realized, "or it could mean absolutely nothing—just be a coincidence."

Nevertheless, she was so disturbed that she considered tiptoeing downstairs and telephoning Tom Reese about this enigmatic evening.

"Oh, bother! Tom goes away every week end. I can't reach him until the week end is over. And Mrs. Julian, too, is out of town."

The question would have to wait. Anyway, did she or didn't she have anything worth telling?

CHAPTER X

Where the Melody Led

WHEN CHERRY ARRIVED AT THE MEDICAL DEPART-
ment on Monday at two P.M., to work on the late
shift until nine P.M., she found her assistant excited.

"What's happened here this morning, Gladys? If
it was urgent, why didn't you phone me?"

"It didn't happen in the medical department, Miss
Ames, but it happened on this floor and the whole
store's buzzing about it! It's only a rumor, but it's all
very strange!"

"Don't keep me in suspense," Cherry said. "Come
on in while I change into my uniform."

"Well, Miss Ames, it seems that music box of
Mrs. Julian's is—not exactly missing, but misplaced.
Though how it could be misplaced, goodness knows!
And after those two other thefts—"

Cherry's fingers froze on the buttons of her white

140

uniform. She asked Gladys who had reported that the music box was misplaced.

"The rumor says that Mr. Dance reported it."

Cherry did not like the sound of all this. Misplaced? That was hard to believe after what she had heard on the road leading to Woodacres—to the Otto Galleries. Mr. Otto himself had handled the music box last Tuesday afternoon, at the special exhibit and lecture.

"Gladys, when was the music box last seen?"

"I don't know. Nobody seems to know."

"Or maybe somebody does know. Let's skip that. Did you hear when Mr. Dance reported that the music box was misplaced?"

"Saturday evening, late, after you'd left the store at five, Miss Ames! I hear he said he didn't realize at first that it was misplaced."

"Hmm. Wonder why it took Mr. Dance from Tuesday afternoon until late Saturday to discover and report that the music box couldn't be found," Cherry said half to herself.

"It looks like a third theft, doesn't it, Miss Ames?"

"I'm afraid it could be that. Thanks for telling me, Gladys. Do you want to man the desk while I put on my white shoes and stockings? Then you're free to go to lunch."

The first thing Cherry did, after attending to routine duties for an hour, and then two patients, was to go next door and ask for Mr. Reese. The secretary, Miss Josephson, eyed Cherry with unblinking owl-like calm.

"Mr. Reese won't be able to see you—or anybody —this afternoon, Miss Ames. Trouble's poppin' in our Philadelphia store and he's tied up on a long-distance call."

"Then will you put me down for an appointment for tomorrow, please? Thanks, Miss Josephson."

The next day seemed to Cherry an eternity of minor nursing chores, routine records, and those necessary delays, eating and sleeping, before the hour for her appointment with Tom Reese rolled around.

They met, at her request, in his office for greater privacy. Today Tom looked hard-pressed, not at all like the gay young man of a few evenings past.

"Hello, Cherry. What can I do for you?" He pulled up a chair for her, and grinned. "Wow, what a time we've been having! I may have to run down to Philadelphia and straighten out a procedural tangle. Hope not—enough to do here. How are you, anyway?"

"Good, thanks, except that I'm troubled about Mrs. Julian's music box."

"Come to the point."

"As if you'd let anyone hem and haw! All right, I think the music box has been stolen, not misplaced."

"Me, too. That's off the record, Cherry, because nothing definite has been learned yet. The store detectives and also the insurance company's men are turning the store inside out. And they've been questioning Dance. But nothing definite has turned up so far."

"And do the detectives still suspect Mrs. Julian about the Ming vase, even though her music box has been taken?"

"Misplaced," Tom corrected her, but his voice was ironical. "Yes, they still suspect Mrs. Julian. I gather that's because their investigators haven't as yet been able to turn up any other suspect—for the highboy theft, either."

"I still think she's incapable of stealing," Cherry said stubbornly.

Tom sighed and shrugged. He glanced sidelong at his wrist watch, then looked guilty as Cherry caught him at it.

"I know I'm taking up valuable time," she said. "Tom, just *when* was the music box stolen or misplaced?"

"That's the crux of the question."

Quickly he summed up what facts he knew. The music box was last seen by several persons a week ago this afternoon, when Mr. Otto lectured and held it up to view. Cherry mentioned that the music box had been passed around among the audience.

"It might have vanished at that point," Tom conceded. "But don't you think Mrs. Julian would have wondered where it was? Don't you think Miss Lamb and old Heller, and the store detectives on special duty that afternoon, all had their eyes fixed on it while the music box circulated?"

Cherry nodded. "It must have come back to the lecturer's table."

"And that was in full view of the audience."

The lecturer's table flashed into Cherry's mind's eye, with the porcelain plates and the Georgian silver and Mr. Otto's large brief case upon it as Otto talked. Then she focused on Tom again, and came back to the present.

"Tom, something you said just now—what was it? Oh, yes, why didn't Mrs. Julian wonder where her music box was?"

"Well, of course, it may not have been misplaced or stolen until Thursday or Friday or Saturday, *after* she left on her trip."

A comment of Mrs. Julian's returned to Cherry with unexpected force. She repeated to Tom Reese how the woman had described Mr. Dance's system of putting certain wanted items away in the closet, to whet a customer's interest into actual buying.

"Does he? That's clever merchandising," Tom commented. "Dance said that he had locked it in the closet late Tuesday afternoon, but I assumed that was for safekeeping—not a merchandising gimmick."

"Well, maybe the music box was put in the closet then," Cherry said thoughtfully. "Mrs. Julian seemed to think so. But what I want to know is why Dance didn't discover until Saturday that it was misplaced?"

"Theoretically, it could have been an honest oversight," Tom replied. "He said that he looked for the music box Saturday afternoon, couldn't find it, ransacked the entire antiques department, still couldn't find it. So Saturday evening he reported that it was misplaced."

"But why," Cherry asked, "did Mr. Dance consider it misplaced rather than missing or stolen?"

"He said he had locked the closet after the lecture on Tuesday, and only he has the key. The detectives examined the closet lock. It hadn't been picked, and they didn't find any fingerprints."

"Well, what do the detectives think of Dance in the face of such a story?"

"They are inclined to look on him as one of those artistic, impractical people who are a bit absent-minded. Pierce thinks the music box is only misplaced and will turn up sooner or later. Thinks Dance carefully put it away and has forgotten where."

"But do you believe that's what happened?"

"I did at first, but talking to you has given me an

entirely new perspective on the whole matter, especially so far as Dance is concerned. He's shrewd as a hawk and it's difficult to believe that he wouldn't have noticed that the music box wasn't where it was supposed to be. Unless, of course, it wasn't taken until shortly before he looked for it on Saturday. But that still doesn't account for the lack of fingerprints, does it?"

Cherry didn't answer Tom's question. Instead, she countered with one of her own.

"And isn't it rather strange that Dance suddenly decided to send Mrs. Julian on her first buying trip last week? If she had been here, she might have inquired about the music box. Do you think it all ties in?"

"It could, but we need facts, Cherry—hard, cold facts." Tom went on to say that he was considering whether to write Mrs. Julian about the missing music box.

"Bad news can wait, and Mrs. Julian has enough worries already," Cherry said.

"All right. No letter."

This time it was Cherry who glanced at her wrist watch. She stood up to go.

"I just hope," she said, "that before Mrs. Julian comes back, we'll have solved the thefts and cleared her. I hope we'll have recovered her music box by then, poor woman."

"I'm not optimistic," Tom said. "Do you have something more on your mind? Don't rush off. Let's spend another five minutes and thresh this thing out."

Cherry said, "Thanks," and sat down again. She had wanted to tell Tom Reese about the whistler on the road to Woodacres, whistling a few bars of the telltale minuet. Yet here in broad daylight, in a business office, the incident seemed thin and dubious. What was there to tell? The person whistling could have heard the melody when Mr. Otto played the music box last Tuesday afternoon for the audience, and half memorized the tune. Even if the whistler were Otto, the explanation could be that simple. Tom might laugh if she told him such a slight, dreamlike thing.

"Well? You're awfully quiet, Cherry."

"Tom, do you know whether Mr. Otto was in the store Saturday, when the theft either occurred or was discovered?"

"So far as I know, he wasn't," Tom said. "The detectives checked back on who was in and out of the antiques department on Saturday. I saw their list. Of course even Pierce isn't infallible—but he sure is dogged."

"The one who's so set against Mrs. Julian," Cherry murmured. "I wish you'd tell this Detective Pierce about an incident between Dance and Otto—"

She recounted to Tom how agitated Mr. Dance had become when Otto telephoned him at the store, particularly when one of the staff answered the phone.

Tom didn't comment, but he nodded and made a note.

They talked a bit about the cleverness of the thief or thieves, whoever they were, for in each of the three thefts, the thieves had used a different technique. The tiny Ming vase had disappeared off a counter practically under Mrs. Julian's very eyes. The immense highboy had been stolen by a clever trick. And now the music box was rather belatedly reported misplaced.

"I'd think it fair to deduce," Tom said, "that one or more of the thieves is a bona fide art expert. On the highboy theft, at least, I'd guess more than one person was in on it. It certainly is beginning to look as if someone inside the antiques department—" His telephone rang. Tom leaned toward it. . . . "This call is probably from Philadelphia. We'll talk some more later, Cherry. . . . Hello, Reese speaking. . . . Yes, go ahead."

Cherry rose, waved, and left his office.

At five Gladys left for the day. Cherry would remain on duty until nine. After a flurry of activity between six and seven, she had a lull in which to send for a sandwich and do some thinking.

It might be a good idea to talk with Mr. Dance and hear directly from him this "misplaced" story. The antiques department could not be very busy, now that it was nearly nine P.M. Cherry crossed the corridor, figuring she could keep an eye on the medical department for a few minutes from here.

Miss Janet Lamb came up to her. Cherry inquired whether Mr. Dance was there this evening.

"Why, no, Miss Ames, he hasn't been in the store all day. That happens sometimes when he's out buying. Do you want me to tell Mr. Dance you were looking for him? Did you wish to see him about anything special?"

Cherry recognized with a start that a nurse in white uniform making frequent visits to the antiques department might indeed look odd.

"Never mind, thanks, Miss Lamb," Cherry said hastily, and retreated to her own domain.

On Wednesday, and for the balance of the week, Cherry would be on the early shift. It was shortly after store opening that Mr. Dance strolled over to the open door of the medical department and said:

"Good morning, Miss Ames. I understand you were looking for me?"

His smile was as bland as ever, and he looked exceedingly sleek and well this morning.

"Why—ah—yes, I was, Mr. Dance." Cherry was

taken by surprise. She said the first innocuous thing that came into her head. "I was wondering if you had heard from Mrs. Julian?"

"Now why do you ask that?" His smile was indulgent, but his eyes did not smile. "Oh, no need to tell me. You're concerned about her health, I know, and it's very good indeed of you."

Mr. Dance chatted on, saying naturally Mrs. Julian was keeping in touch with him, she was well, she had bought a very interesting old melodeon, the department missed her.

"He talks a lot but tells nothing," Cherry observed to herself.

"I'm glad to hear good news of Mrs. Julian," she said aloud.

"You've heard the unfortunate news about her music box? Poor lady, I haven't had the heart to tell her yet. I can't tell you how much I regret its being misplaced. How badly I feel."

"Perhaps it will turn up safely."

Dance shrugged. "One hopes so." Then, his regrets expressed, he grew cheerful again. "It isn't really so bad for Mrs. Julian, you know. She'll receive insurance compensation payment for it."

Cherry was thinking. Willard Dance would have to pay the insurance company for the highboy, but he also was liable to repay the full value of the music box. He certainly seemed unworried, even blithe, at the prospect of having to pay the insurance company another several hundred dollars in case the music box did not turn up. He didn't mention it, either.

"So you see, Miss Ames, you mustn't concern yourself *too* much about Mrs. Julian. It isn't necessary or even wise of you."

"I only meant that she'd feel distressed to learn— Why, what do you mean, 'not wise,' Mr. Dance?"

He said gently, "I feel sure your loyalty to Anna Julian is as complete as mine. If it weren't, I would never mention anything so prejudicial. However, *entre nous*, Miss Ames, don't you see how unfortunately, in another respect, this incident works out for her?"

"No, I don't. She isn't even here!"

"Ah, exactly, that's the point. Mrs. Julian goes out of town, then I discover her music box is missing, then she collects a nice fat insurance payment for it." He made a wry, amused face. "I'm sure the insurance compensation at the item's full value will bring her more money than what we could sell the music box for. That is, assuming we could sell it for her. Now, then, do you think that looks *well* for her?"

Cherry's mind was reeling. "Do you mean to hint, Mr. Dance, that Mrs. Julian deliberately took the music box herself?"

He drew a long breath and looked at her sadly. "That's precisely what some of the investigators are thinking. They entertain a suspicion, and it hurts me to speak so bluntly of our friend."

"But that's fantastic!" Cherry exclaimed.

"Is it? She is already suspect in the theft of the Ming vase. She *was* present and had the key on the afternoon of the guest speakers. May I remind you that was the last afternoon anyone remembers seeing the music box. Of course I can't say how deeply I regret—"

"But on that afternoon it could just as well have been—" Cherry stopped short.

"I beg your pardon, Miss Ames?"

Dance was eying her. Cherry decided to keep quiet. She was so angry she wanted to blurt out that Mr. Otto, too, had handled the music box that afternoon and could have taken it. Or Dance himself could have quietly slipped it out of the department, with no one the wiser. But a sense of caution warned her to hold her tongue. After all, she might be dealing with dangerous men. Better not let Dance guess what she was thinking and planning to do.

For a plan was already crystallizing, as Mr. Dance made a few more bland remarks and returned to his gallery across the corridor.

Cherry could scarcely wait for a chance to visit Woodacres and get inside the house. She had better act fast; she had better *make* an opportunity. A good thing she was on the early shift for the next few days.

"But, Cherry," said Aunt Kathy that evening, "I don't see how you'll ever gain entrance to the Otto Galleries. If Mr. Otto recognizes you as the store nurse—"

"You just said you'll help me, Aunt Kathy. Won't you?"

Gwen said crossly, "I think you're both about to do something you may be sorry for. I'm surprised at you, Aunt Kathy."

"Now, Gwen, I'm old enough to know what I'm doing. I *am* fascinated by this provoking situation, and what's more, I feel as responsible for Cherry as I do for you. You are both guests in my house, under my chaperonage."

Gwen grumbled but said only that she, at least, wanted no part of the escapade. She wandered off into another room with a magazine.

"Well, Cherry, I understand that invitation read *By Appointment*. And it was sent only to certain persons, not to everyone."

"An invitation was sent to Mrs. McIntosh, who's Betty Lane's employer." Cherry set aside the Christmas gifts for her family which she had shopped for early, and all of them were wrapping. "Mmm. Do you suppose you could pretend to be Mrs. McIntosh?

No, that isn't ethical," she corrected herself. "Well, then, could you and I be acquaintances of Mrs. McIntosh, through whom you'd heard of the Otto Galleries? Acquaintances of Betty Lane's, too."

"That's stretching the truth," Aunt Kathy said hesitantly, "but I don't believe it would give any injury or offense to Mrs. McIntosh, which is what I'm concerned about. Very well, Cherry, *suppose* I presented myself at Otto Galleries as an acquaintance of Mrs. McIntosh?"

"They'd let you in. And I'd come in with you, with my eyes and ears wide open."

"I'm beginning to see. But we'd need an appointment."

"If you're willing," Cherry said, "you could telephone for an appointment tomorrow morning. Ask for sometime late in the afternoon, either tomorrow or Friday."

She added that the late hours of the afternoon, five to seven, often were the busiest in Mr. Dance's gallery, for instance, when businessmen with the means to buy art objects came in with their wives. That was probably true of many or most galleries during the Christmas season.

"Late tomorrow or Friday afternoon," Aunt Kathy repeated. "I'll do it."

They decided Kathy Martin had better not give her own name. As for the remote chance that Otto might note and trace the license plates on Aunt Kathy's car, that was a chance they would have to take.

On Thursday, Cherry reported to work at nine A.M., took no lunch hour but worked right through, and thus was able to leave the store at four P.M. By hurrying, she just caught a Long Island train, an express. It was a little before five when she ran up the driveway to the Martin's house.

Aunt Kathy was ready, wearing a hat for a change, and waiting in her car.

"Do I look presentable?" Cherry panted. "Did you get an appointment all right?"

"Everything's fine. Get in, Cherry. It will take us half an hour to get over there, so we'd better start."

In the waning daylight of a December afternoon, North Road looked bare, and the trees as gaunt as black skeletons. Woodacres, when they reached it, seemed to have shrunk in daylight. The house was fairly large, run-down; only a trace of a driveway remained. Once this must have been an imposing estate. The house stood in the midst of wooded grounds and undergrowth made parking difficult.

"Now don't forget, you're Mrs. Hunt, and I'm your niece. I won't give my name at all unless I have to."

The two climbed the broad steps to the front door,

and Cherry rang the bell. After a moment's wait, a woman opened the door.

Cherry had to restrain herself from clutching at Aunt Kathy's arm. This was the tall, stout, ungainly woman of the train who had marked the newspaper! Luckily, Aunt Kathy was talking smoothly, and the woman answered, "Yes, we were expecting you, Mrs. Hunt. I am Mrs. Otto. So nice of Mrs. McIntosh and her Miss Lane to tell you about our gallery."

So the woman was Mrs. Otto! Cherry followed blindly after the two women into a display room. Why hadn't she realized that Otto, big, lumbering, bulky, and this big woman—both middle-aged, both in the same severe, drab sort of clothes—were two of a kind?

"Is there something special you are interested in, Mrs. Hunt?"

"Why, yes, I'm looking for old clocks," Aunt Kathy said as prearranged, "and I'm very much interested in finding a good, small inlaid table, too."

The pattern was falling into place for Cherry. If the newspaper markings were a code—Dance had said he'd told Otto repeatedly not to telephone him, especially at the store—then Mrs. Otto had been serving as messenger and go-between. "So that's why I saw her commuting between Long Island and the city—and why I saw her in the store!"

But these thoughts were brushed away as Cherry

heard, very faintly, the tinkle of a music box. The same plaintive minuet! It seemed to come from an adjoining room, and it sounded muffled as if something, a coat or rug, had been thrown over the music box.

"Oh, what have I walked into! And where is Mr. Otto? Why isn't he here in the display room?"

The women discussed a clock, and Cherry listened to the melody of the music box. Knowing the tune pretty well by this time, she recognized that the disc, which ran for about seven minutes, was playing its last repeat chorus and was nearly at its end. Someone must have started the music-box mechanism in motion just as she and Aunt Kathy were driving up to the house, and it could not be stopped.

The melody was ending. The faint tinkle stopped.

"Mrs. Otto," Cherry said, trying not to let her voice tremble, "what a pretty little music box tune that was! It sounded like"—she must not say Mrs. Julian's —"like one of those old German music boxes, made around the end of the eighteenth century. It must be a lovely one."

"Yes, it is lovely but you are mistaken, my dear young lady, about its type. It is a French music box, made about 1850."

Did she imagine that the woman's high-colored face grew still more flushed? Cherry did not dare meet Aunt Kathy's eyes.

"Well, French or German," Cherry said, forcing a smile, "I'd love to see it."

"Oh, I'm afraid not. It's one that a customer requested, and we are holding it for him. So I really do not have the right to show it for sale, you see?"

"I only want to admire it, Mrs. Otto—"

Aunt Kathy broke in quickly, almost warningly. "Now dear, Mrs. Otto is right. Don't coax. There are enough beautiful things in this room for you to admire."

"Yes! Yes, indeed," said Mrs. Otto. "Won't you and your niece come look at this clock? Hand-carved, and it chimes—perhaps I can make it sound the hour for you. I am sorry, Mrs. Hunt, that we do not have very many things to show you this afternoon, but the Otto Galleries at Woodacres is a new venture for us."

"Do you have another display room?" Aunt Kathy asked, quite naturally. Cherry could have hugged her.

"Just this one room, Mrs. Hunt, so far. It was our living room. These old houses are large, but the layouts are badly planned. We hope to put in better lighting; this chandelier does not do justice to the paintings. Did you see these small ones?"

The woman tried hard to sell them a group of miniature paintings. She insisted that the visitors take them in their hands to examine them closely. Cherry set down her purse and gloves on a table; the paintings, tiny, enchanting, Watteau-like landscapes, were marvels of painting skill when seen at close range.

But why did the music box remain silent? Where was Mr. Otto? What person or persons were behind the closed door? Or was no one in there? Mrs. Otto herself might have played the music box for her own pleasure.

"The miniatures are perfect beauties," Aunt Kathy was saying to Mrs. Otto, "but before making such an extravagant purchase, I should like to think it over and perhaps talk it over with my husband."

"Yes, naturally, but you must not say 'extravagant.' You will enjoy them many years."

"Well, we appreciate your letting us see them, and your other beautiful things. Come, dear," she said to Cherry. "We've taken quite enough of Mrs. Otto's time."

Cherry, too, was eager to get out of this house. But Mrs. Otto, escorting them to the door, was in no hurry.

"Why don't I hold the miniatures for you for a few days? It would be a shame for you to decide you want them, and then find they have been sold."

From the recesses of the house—from behind that closed door?—Cherry distinctly heard the click of a telephone being dialed.

"—considerate of you, Mrs. Otto, but I don't want

to rob you of a sale. Suppose I decide within a day
or two, and telephone you?"

Yes, it was a telephone being dialed, but no sound
of anyone speaking yet. Sometimes a call to the city
took a few minutes to be put through.

"Good-by then, Mrs. Otto," said Aunt Kathy, "and
thank you."

"Good-by, and thank you both for coming." Mrs.
Otto opened the door and remarked what a mild
evening it was. "I'll leave the door ajar. A house
gets so stuffy with the heat on. Be careful of the
steps, ladies."

Just as she and Aunt Kathy reached their car,
Cherry realized she had forgotten her gloves. She
murmured to Aunt Kathy that she'd left them on a
table in the display room. They were her best French
gloves, and a gift from her mother.

"Don't go back in there, Cherry! Don't force your
luck."

Cherry hesitated. She wanted her gloves, and she
wanted very much to hear that telephone conversation. She still felt unsatisfied with the visit and Mrs.
Otto's explanation of the music box.

"I'll be quick."

She left Aunt Kathy and ran noiselessly up the
steps, hoping the gathering dusk would hide her.
She slipped just inside the door, into the hallway.

Standing there, her heart pounding so hard she

felt nearly suffocated, Cherry heard Otto's voice. It came loud and clear—that door must be open now—and he was obviously speaking to someone on the telephone.

"Listen, I *had* to call you up. I know you don't like it—"

A pause. Otto must be listening. Cherry stepped back deeper into the hallway. Mrs. Otto had turned on the ceiling light here and it shone down on her. At least, the display room was empty, for the moment.

"Listen, Dance, I did try to stop it, but you know these old notched-disc mechanisms! Once you set one in motion, it automatically plays its allotted minutes and can't be stopped without jamming or breaking it. . . . What? . . . Don't be a fool, Dance! We would never find a craftsman who could repair it properly, not in this country. . . . What? How could I take it upstairs without being seen from the display room?"

Then Otto seemed to explode. Dance must have asked him why he needed to stop the music box from playing.

"Because just when I start to play it for my own pleasure, who drives in but a woman bringing that nosy nurse from the store! . . . Yes, you hear right! I look through the window to see what customers are coming and I see the nurse. So I run and grab the music box out of the display room. No, I am not mistaken about the Ames girl! . . . What makes you think she doesn't know the tune? I muffled it with my coat, but for the full seven minutes it— What? What? . . . How do I know what she's up to? You know her better than I do—"

Then apparently Otto listened. But not for long. He exploded again.

"Dance, you are a fool. Of course, I know she is a friend of Julian's! . . . No, Minna didn't know who the girl was. She knows now." Otto's voice was bitter.

"I'd better go," Cherry thought. *"I'd better get out of here while I still can. This is a dangerous place for me."*

Just as she turned toward the door, she saw, out of the corner of her eye, Mrs. Otto walk into the display room.

"Cherry Ames!" Mrs. Otto cried out loudly. "I thought you were gone!"

"My gloves," Cherry stammered. She darted into the display room and seized them, an excuse no longer mattered, then flew out, down the steps, and almost flung herself into the car. The engine was running.

"Aunt Kathy! We've got to get out of here fast!"

They pulled out in seconds and streaked along North Road toward the traffic circle. Cherry turned around several times, but no one was following them.

"Whew! I don't know what Otto would have done

to me. I only know that house isn't a healthy place for me!"

"I told you to leave well enough alone. What happened?"

Cherry told Aunt Kathy. To her surprise, Aunt Kathy did not scold. In fact, she felt as Cherry did, that those few risky minutes spent in the hallway yielded definitive information.

"Yes," said Cherry sadly, "but I still haven't any evidence. I mean, concrete evidence that would stand up in a court of law."

"You've learned what you needed to know," Aunt Kathy reminded her.

"I don't underestimate that, and I certainly do thank you for undertaking this visit. *But* we still need proof."

"Isn't the presence of the music box in the Otto Galleries proof enough?"

"It would be if the detectives or police walked in and found it there. But now that Otto and Dance know I'm on to them, what's to prevent them from removing the music box from Woodacres?"

"Then it would be their word against yours," said Aunt Kathy. "See here, Cherry. Maybe your friend Tom Reese would know what to do."

Cherry brightened. "I'll call him at the store the instant we reach home."

Fifteen minutes later she had made connections

with the Thomas and Parke switchboard. Miss Josephson, Tom's secretary, answered.

"No, Miss Ames, Mr. Reese isn't here. . . . No, you can't reach him anywhere else, because he left in a hurry for Philadelphia this afternoon. You know about the tangle down there? Right in the midst of the Christmas sales? He's gone down there to trouble-shoot—"

Cherry murmured the bad news to Aunt Kathy. She urged Cherry to secure the telephone number of the Philadelphia store.

"I'm sorry, Miss Ames, but you'd be wasting your time to phone down there. Mr. Reese will be too busy with the local mess to give any time to New York calls. Can't it wait? Or can't I help you? Or can't somebody else here in the store manager's office help you?"

Cherry explained that her business was highly confidential and only for Tom Reese's ears. She could hear Miss Josephson sniff; as Tom's personal secretary, she resented any secrets. Cherry asked when he would return.

"Mr. Reese will be in the store on Monday morning. . . . No, not before, Miss Ames. He will be in Philadelphia through Saturday, and then up to Connecticut for Sunday as usual. . . . No, I am not at liberty to give you the Connecticut telephone number. . . . Really, Miss Ames! Good-by!"

Click went the receiver as Miss Josephson indignantly hung up.

All Cherry could do now was wait. That was not easy. A few days' time would give Otto and Dance a chance to cover up their guilt or take new action. It was not comfortable to wait, either, knowing that she was in some degree of danger. To wait—how senseless! Yet Cherry was stumped as to what her next move should be.

~~~~~~~~~~~~~~~~~

CHAPTER XI

The Rose Diamond Necklace

"WHAT A CROWD!" CHERRY SAID TO THREE OTHER girls who couldn't get into the employees' entrance on Monday morning. This was December twenty-fourth, the last shopping day before Christmas, and the customers blocked all doors. "The store will be a madhouse today!"

"Brace yourself." One of the girls smiled at her. "It'll be hectic. At least we close at five this evening."

"Please let us through!" a man in back of Cherry shouted.

Everyone felt gay this morning, though. Who wouldn't with Christmas only a day off? Even the bitter cold and the gray day couldn't dampen spirits. "We'll have snow yet," someone said hopefully.

At last, laughing about their difficulties, the store people managed to squeeze their way through the crowd of waiting customers and enter the building.

Cherry was in the medical department before her assistant—both nurses would be on duty all day today—and found the morning's mail and memoranda already delivered to her desk. Cherry half looked for a post card from Tom Reese, sent from Philadelphia last week, just for fun, but apparently he had been too busy.

"Hello, what's this?"

Cherry found a letter for her from Boston, handwritten on hotel stationery. The graceful penmanship looked familiar, but Cherry could not place it. She opened the envelope and glanced at the bottom of the letter. It was signed "Anna Julian."

> "Dear Cherry: Just a brief note to advise you that my business is completed, and I will be back in New York a little sooner than Mr. Dance has scheduled me to return. Perhaps I shall be home by late Monday afternoon, the 24th. I do not plan to notify Mr. Dance of my slightly earlier return."

Cherry understood that she was not to notify him, either. She resumed reading the letter.

> "During this week in Boston, I inquired at the headquarters of the antiques dealers' association and spoke to two persons, separately. Both knew Elbert Otto slightly as a long-time art consultant. It seems he was competent enough but has held rather obscure, minor jobs with various art-gallery owners. Both men here in-

timated to me that Mr. Otto has been involved in at least one questionable transaction.

"As for Willard Dance, I was disappointed to learn that he is not a member of the association. In fact, the antiques dealers as a group had never heard of him until his dealings with Thomas and Parke. Not that this is any reflection on Mr. Dance, of course—as you know, he was formerly in the precious jewelry business.

"I trust this information will be interesting to you. With thanks again for all your kindness to me, I am,

Most sincerely yours,

Anna Julian"

Interesting? It certainly was interesting information! Though not greatly significant in itself, this news of Otto's and Dance's lack of professional standing fit into the over-all picture. As for Otto's having been involved in a shady deal before, that was not surprising after having discovered the "misplaced" music box out on Long Island.

Cherry was eager to tell Tom Reese about what she had learned at Woodacres, and now Mrs. Julian's letter. She went next door, hoping Tom's door might be standing open.

It was shut. She had to confront his secretary. Miss Josephson blinked at her calmly from behind those owllike glasses.

"You're wasting your time, Miss Ames. He's up to his ears in emergencies."

"But this is urgent, too," Cherry insisted.

"Can't *I* take your message?"

Cherry tried to smooth her feelings by explaining that her information involved other persons for whom she had no right to speak. "Besides, Miss Josephson, it's such a long and complicated matter, it would take me perhaps half an hour to brief you on it."

"Very well." The secretary looked mollified. "I'll ring your phone as soon as Mr. Reese is free. But it won't be soon. He has to see those men who are investigating the highboy theft."

"Thank you," and Cherry left the store manager's office. She was reluctant to take action without Tom's advice.

Cherry returned to the medical department. Gladys Green was on duty, and nothing much was happening.

Cherry had an idea. Suppose she mentioned to Mr. Dance her visit to the Otto Galleries? It might be revealing to watch his reaction.

"Gladys, I'm going to look for Mr. Dance. Call me if you need me."

She made it a point to avoid Miss Janet Lamb this morning—goodhearted, but so talkative. Since Mr. Dance was not in sight, Cherry sought out old Adam Heller.

"Good morning, Miss Ames. You look as fresh as a red rose this morning," he said.

"Thank you. You're the only courtly man I know, Mr. Heller. Is Mr. Dance available?"

"Mr. Dance isn't here."

"Oh. Well, later then."

"No, Miss Ames, I'm afraid not. Mr. Dance does not plan to come into the store at all today. He telephoned a few minutes ago that he is ill."

"That's too bad," Cherry said, not because of sympathy for Willard Dance. "I did want to see him."

Then she noticed her assistant signaling from the doorway. Cherry excused herself and sped across the corridor to find that five people had come into the medical department at once. One of them was Santa Claus. "The ventilating system in the toy department has broken down and besides I have a toothache," Santa reported. Cherry gave him a dental poultice and an aspirin. The other four cases ranged from an upset stomach to a smashed finger to a particle in a boy's eye. All were small injuries, but unless first aid were given promptly and correctly, these people could become seriously sick.

Busy as she was, Cherry jumped slightly whenever the telephone rang. But not once was it Miss Josephson or Tom Reese. There was no chance to catch him at lunch hour, because Cherry and her assistant worked straight through the twelve-to-one and one-to-two periods.

Finally, at nearly three, Cherry had a few free

minutes. Wise of her or not, she went next door to check with Miss Josephson. On the last day before Christmas, even the secretary's calm was wobbling.

"I can't find anybody!" she greeted Cherry. "Two hours ago I heard Tom Reese was in the warehouse, but I haven't been able to locate him since! And I have a stack of messages for him, all urgent."

"I can see another message for him is just what you don't need," Cherry remarked.

"Oh, I'll have him get in touch with you—if I can ever find him!"

Cherry worked hard the rest of that afternoon. Patients coming in, mostly with fatigue headaches, described for her the last-minute bedlam on other floors. Late in the afternoon a customer who had fainted was brought in, in a wheel chair, a floor supervisor pushing it.

"Miss Ames, this lady tells me she has a heart condition. Take care of her, will you?"

"Is there identification in her purse?" Cherry asked. "I'd better telephone someone in her family. Gladys, help her onto a cot."

But first the woman, overhearing, weakly told them the name and office telephone number of her son. "Jack will come for me. Don't alarm him, though, please."

"Shall I telephone?" the floor supervisor asked.

"Thanks, but I'd rather check her over first," and Cherry, with Gladys' help, gently, gradually, placed the woman on a cot in the adjoining room.

Cherry checked carefully but found nothing seriously wrong. Apparently, in the crowd and close air and excitement, Mrs. Guthrie had come close to a heart attack but had not actually suffered one. Cherry asked the woman for her doctor's diagnosis of her condition, and what treatment or medication or diet, if any, he prescribed for her. Knowing this, Cherry was able to decide that Mrs. Guthrie did not need a doctor's immediate services, and that the best thing for her for the next hour would be to rest and be quiet.

"Do you think you can go to sleep, Mrs. Guthrie?" Cherry asked, covering her with blankets. "Then I think you'll have enough strength to go home, providing your son takes you in a car or taxi."

"He will. But I'm afraid, Nurse, that my son will be delayed. He's an outside man and he doesn't report back to his office before five or five thirty. Besides, Jack told me his customers will be giving office parties, Christmas Eve parties, late this afternoon."

"Don't worry. I'll be right here with you, or just in the next room, no matter how long your son may be delayed. Now try to sleep, Mrs. Guthrie. Comfortable?"

"Yes, thank you, Nurse."

Cherry tiptoed out, closed the door for quiet, and telephoned the son's office. She left a message for Jack Guthrie, and was careful to add that he need have no cause for alarm.

Mrs. Guthrie slept, and the business day drew to a close. Five o'clock was closing time on Christmas Eve. At five Gladys offered to stay on, if Cherry wished, but added wistfully that she was giving a Christmas Eve party at her house that evening. "But if you need me—"

"No, that's all right, Gladys. Thanks just the same."

Gladys's party suddenly reminded Cherry that the Spencer Club nurses were having a Christmas Eve party, too, this evening at No. 9. She planned to stay there overnight, then fly to Hilton early tomorrow. And hadn't Tom Reese said something about a Christmas Eve date?

"Can you keep an eye on Mrs. Guthrie for just a few minutes?" Cherry asked as Gladys was putting on her coat.

Cherry hurried next door to see Miss Josephson, who sat limp and beaten at her desk.

"He's still not here, Miss Ames. Now he's tied up in a meeting in the store president's office. I did give Mr. Reese your message but— I'm awfully sorry."

"Well, will you give him this letter?" Cherry handed the secretary Mrs. Julian's letter. It was the best she could do. "And will you please tell him I still need to talk to him?"

"I may not see him, Miss Ames, because I'm going home soon, and if I leave a note he might overlook it. Why don't I give you Mr. Reese's home telephone number? I know that he's planning to go out to dinner this evening, but you could surely reach him at home between six and seven."

The secretary wrote down Tom Reese's home telephone number and Cherry put it in her purse. They wished each other "Merry Christmas," and Cherry returned to the clinic.

"Well, now you're free, Gladys. I hope you have a nice party with your friends."

"Thanks. I hate leaving you here, Miss Ames. Are you sure you don't need me? Good night, then, and Merry Christmas."

After Gladys and most of the other employees on this floor had left, it grew very quiet. Cherry went in to see her patient who was awake now. Cherry helped her to sit up, and gave her a bracing cup of very hot tea.

At a quarter to six a young man appeared worriedly at the door of the medical department. Cherry explained to him what had happened, and emphasized the need for a taxi, and more bed rest for his mother this evening.

"Yes, Nurse. And do you think her doctor should see her?"

"It might be a good idea, particularly if it would put your mind at ease. She seems to be all right again, though."

Cherry walked them to the bank of elevators at the end of the floor. The store was closed now, the elevators and escalators were closed down, only the night elevator was running. After some delay it came up for the Guthries, who thanked the nurse profusely.

Cherry hurried back along the deserted sixth floor. She wanted to get out of here before most of the lights went off. Someone was locking up the personnel office and its records. No one was in the antiques department, with its locked cases, and the store manager's office was already dark. Cherry changed rapidly into street clothes, quickly checked up to see that she was leaving everything in good order, and hurried along to the night elevator.

There she waited an exasperating five minutes. So much to do when she reached No. 9—shower and change, and Bertha might need a helper with the refreshments. If she could reach Tom Reese at his house, she'd invite him to stop by at No. 9 later. Thank goodness, here came the elevator.

It was after six by the time Cherry got out of the store and onto the street. She hurried along in the cold, skirting the edges of the home-going crowd. Which would be less crowded, bus or subway? She was debating this when a man coming from the other direction caught her eye.

It was Willard Dance. He certainly was in a great hurry. Why, he was supposed to be ill today! Dance did not look at all ill, just as dapper as usual, and what's more, he seemed to be heading for the store. At this hour?

Cherry wheeled around. If he were going into the store after hours, she wanted to know what for. She hesitated only a moment, then followed him. She almost had to run after Dance.

He went directly to the side door where a watchman was on duty to let out the last stragglers. Dance held up a card in front of the glass door, the watchman admitted him, and he disappeared from Cherry's view. She ran and at the same time dug in her handbag for her own identification. The watchman let her in just as the night elevator rose upward.

"Is there any other elevator running?" Cherry demanded. "A freight elevator?"

"No, miss."

She watched the indicator rise to the numeral 6, pause there, and the elevator started down again.

Holding her breath, she peered around the pillar

Cherry ran into the car so quickly that she astonished the man who was running it.

"Six, please."

At the sixth floor the door slid noiselessly open and Cherry stepped out. "Don't wait for me," she murmured, and the elevator door closed soundlessly behind her again.

How still it was up here now, how shadowy and dark! She started softly toward the antiques department, unable to see Dance anywhere at first. Then a shadow somewhere ahead of her moved, and she made out his tall figure. Dance was moving swiftly with his back to her. He stopped midway in his gallery. What was he up to?

Cherry stopped, too, behind a pillar, in deep shadows. She heard the faintest of sounds. Was it the click of metal on metal, or a tinkle as something brushed against glass? Holding her breath, she peered around the pillar and saw light glinting and sparkling from something which dangled from Dance's hand. The lid of a display case stood open. The thing caught and reflected what dim light there was—why, it was diamonds—the rose diamond necklace! She saw Dance carefully put it in his inside pocket, then close the lid of the display case. She did not hear him lock the case again. Oh, good heavens, he had turned and was walking rapidly toward her!

A door was standing open and she quickly stepped behind it. Then she trembled for fear she was casting a revealing shadow. Dance passed her as he hurried to the elevator. He was wearing gloves, and apparently had taken the necklace with gloved hands. He pressed the elevator button, then turned nervously, looking in all directions. Had he seen her?

No . . . but she heard someone else coming! Cherry scarcely dared to breathe. Then she saw it was a store guard, going rapidly around a far corner. A second later Dance entered the night elevator.

Cherry fumed as she waited for it to go to the main floor, let him off, and come up again in answer to her ring. How slow could an elevator be? She'd lose him on the street at this rate—Dance seemed to be in an awful rush. And where was he going?

Luckily, the night elevator came right back up for Cherry. She dashed off at the main floor, out of the store, and onto the crowded street. Of all these men in dark overcoats and gray hats, which one was Willard Dance? Suddenly she spotted him getting into a taxi. Taxis were scarce on Christmas Eve in New York; he'd had to wait during those minutes while she'd fumed upstairs. And how long would it take *her* to get a cab?

Cherry waved like mad to passing taxicabs, but they all had fares. Then she saw one pull close to the curb, with someone ready to get out. Cherry waited impatiently while the woman in it paid her fare, then jumped in.

"Do you see that yellow cab ahead?" she said to the driver. "On the inside lane? I want to follow that cab."

"Lady, I don't want any funny business. I don't tail anybody except on a cop's order."

"There's no funny business!" Cherry told him. "It —it's just a little joke on a friend for Christmas Eve. Please!"

"You'd better make it worth my trouble."

"Two-dollar tip," she offered, and the cab spurted ahead.

They were driving north and east through midtown. Where was Dance going? To meet someone? Another thought struck Cherry. Dance, as operator of the antiques department, certainly had a right to come to the store and take away an item of his own department's merchandise, if he wished to do so. He could always say he was taking the necklace to show privately to a customer. Yet what of his hurry, the irregular hour, and above all, his gloved hands? She watched anxiously in the heavy traffic as the two cabs, Dance's and hers, threaded their way.

"Driver, don't lose them!" she called.

"They're pulling over," her driver said over his shoulder. "Better get out your fare if you're in a hurry."

The taxi ahead was stopping alongside a row of tall buildings. From the lighted, curtained windows Cherry could see that these were apartment houses. Cherry's cab stopped at a little distance from Dance's. She saw him step out, but he kept his driver waiting.

"Want me to wait, too?" Cherry's driver asked.

"Well—" If Dance should see a second taxi waiting behind his, with someone waiting in it, he might be suspicious. For this street was half deserted; on Christmas Eve everyone was at home. "No, I'll get out here, driver."

She quickly paid her fare and the tip she had promised, and alighted. Ahead of her Dance was reaching into his pocket, apparently for his door key, and he headed toward a building entrance. The street lamps gave enough illumination for Cherry to see a woman, leaving the building, nod to Dance. He raised his hat; a neighbor probably. He lived here, then. Dance went into the building.

But why was he keeping the taxi waiting? On this dark street she had never seen before, Cherry felt singularly alone. She tried to think what she must do next.

CHAPTER XII

Cherry Gives Chase

~~~~~~~~~~~~~~~~~~~~~~~~~~~~~~~~~~~~~~

IT WAS COLD STANDING THERE FLATTENED AGAINST the building wall, and Cherry was accomplishing nothing. Dance had been gone only two or three minutes, but he might reappear at any time.

"Should I enter the lobby of his apartment building?" Cherry wondered. "And confront him? No, that could be risky. And if I go in and Dance sees me, he'll take every precaution to throw me off his trail."

Cherry noticed a drugstore across the street, at the corner. It had large windows, and she made out a row of telephone booths ranged along the side window. That could be useful to her! If she reached Tom Reese, she could relay this address—but was that enough information to be decisive?

Cherry glanced toward the taxi waiting for Dance. If she could learn something, no matter how little, from the driver— Hoping against hope that Dance would not come out of the building just yet, Cherry ventured over to the parked cab. The driver was bent over, reading a newspaper by the light of the dashboard.

Cherry cleared her throat and the man looked up. "Are you free?" she asked.

"No, lady, I'm waiting for somebody."

"But you haven't a fare. Can't I—"

"Look, lady, I *have* a fare." The driver showed her the card on which all taxi drivers are required to write down their patrons' destination. "See? I'm taking this party out to Idlewild Airport. See where I wrote Idlewild next?"

"All right, thanks."

Idlewild! Cherry knew it was New York's international airfield for transatlantic airlines. Some domestic flights originated at Idlewild, too, but mostly it served passengers going to Europe or the Caribbean or South America. Dance on his way to Idlewild Airport! Did it mean he was leaving the country this evening? It was certain he was fleeing New York. For where?

Cherry walked away into the shadows. For fear the taxi driver would see her loitering, she did not cross the street directly in front of Dance's building. She crossed a bit farther down, rapidly, and ran into the drugstore.

A clerk and two or three customers were in the drugstore. Cherry purchased a package of tooth paste, in order to get change for telephoning, then impatiently hurried to the side and rear of the store. No one else was in the row of telephone booths. She chose the last booth. Was the cab still there? Yes! Through the plate glass she could see the waiting taxi and Dance's lobby entrance, but she probably could be seen only dimly if at all. Cherry was careful to keep the door of the booth open so that the booth light did not snap on, as it did automatically with the door's closing. Then she dropped a coin into the telephone box, and dialed Tom Reese's home number. She kept her eyes fixed on the taxi and doorway diagonally across the street.

"Hello," Tom himself answered. "Hello?"

Cherry breathed a sigh of relief. "Hello, this is Cherry Ames. This is an emergency, Tom. I'm in a drugstore across the street from where Dance lives and—"

"That's a crazy place for you to be on Christmas Eve," Tom said genially. "Haven't we a date later?"

"Yes, we do, but this is no time for socializing. Dance has a taxi waiting. He's going to Idlewild. He just came from the store. I saw him take the rose diamond necklace."

"What!" Tom was instantly serious. "Are you sure? Of both facts?"

"I'm positive. I followed him from the store. What's more, I discovered Otto has the music box. At their house on Long Island called Woodacres, where he and his wife are running a private gallery."

"Whew! Why didn't you tell me this sooner?"

"Because I couldn't reach you! Even today. Have you had a chance to read Mrs. Julian's letter by now?"

"Yes. Sounds suspicious. I have news, too. Listen, Cherry, what are we going to do about this Idlewild move? Do you know where Otto is?"

"Not unless he's upstairs in Dance's building. I'm keeping watch from this booth. But as soon as Dance comes down, I'm going to hail a cab and go directly to Idlewild. I just hope he won't see me before I reach the air—"

Tom made her promise him that she would do nothing on the way to Idlewild or at Idlewild which might jeopardize her safety.

"I'll notify the police before I leave for Idlewild," Tom said, "and I'm leaving immediately. Now you wait for me there, do you hear?"

"Tom!" Cherry gulped into the phone. "Don't hang up. I—I think I see something happening across the street. Hold on—"

A second taxi was stopping behind Dance's cab. A large, heavy man got out, Cherry saw, then a tall, stout, awkward woman.

"Tom, it's the Ottos! Otto and his wife just arrived in a taxi! And they're— Wait—the driver is lifting suitcases out of the taxi for them, and they're carrying extra coats over their arms!"

While Cherry watched, Otto and his driver transferred their luggage into Dance's waiting taxi. Cherry rapidly relayed this to Tom. "So all three of them will—!"

"I'm not surprised," Tom's voice came back dryly. "Things are finally going to get uncomfortable for Dance and Otto. Because of some information I dug up today, the investigators planned to question those two the day after Christmas."

"Day after tomorrow," Cherry repeated. She glanced across the street. Dance had not come downstairs yet; the first cab was still waiting. "Isn't that about the date, if I remember what you told me, when Dance has to pay back to the insurance company for the highboy?"

"That's right. So he's beating it out of the country. With the Ottos. Listen, Cherry, we'd better hang up."

"Yes, it may take me a few minutes to find a taxi. Meet you in the terminal."

"Yes, terminal. Cherry, be careful!" Tom shouted as she replaced the phone.

Cherry chose another door out of the drugstore which led onto a side street, not Dance's street. She would take no chance of letting them see her. She slipped away, rounded a corner, and found herself on a main thoroughfare. A gay party of teen-agers climbed out of one cab, and Cherry hurried to occupy it.

"Idlewild Airport," she instructed the driver. Just as she was climbing into the taxi, she saw a yellow taxi go past her, with three people in it. Dance's cab! This time she did not ask her driver to trail them, but she mustn't lose them!

"Driver, I'm in an awful hurry," she pleaded. "I don't want to miss the plane."

Dance and the Ottos must be caught before their plane took off. If the trio escaped, there was a chance that the thefts would never be solved and Anna Julian would live the rest of her life under a cloud of suspicion.

It was a long ride. In the sea of cars, there were several yellow taxicabs and Cherry could not tell whether one of them was the one she wanted. She mused about what the trio was carrying in those suitcases. It was a safe bet that the rose diamond necklace was still snugly in Dance's pocket. Cherry glanced at her wrist watch as they rode through the gleam of lighted suburbs. What a long ride!

"We're almost there," her driver called cheerfully. "See those hangars and the arc lights across the airfield?"

Now her taxi was swinging up the approach to the airport terminal. Just ahead of her, a yellow taxi was pulling away. Cherry saw Dance and the Ottos walk toward the terminal doors. A porter came up to them, but the men refused to hand over their suitcases. All three people appeared as calm as if they were ordinary travelers, and Mrs. Otto beamed under a hideous hat.

"Well, how'd we do?" Cherry's driver asked proudly. "You going to make your plane?"

"I think so. I certainly am obliged to you, driver."

Cherry paid the meter charges and tipped the man as generously as her depleted purse allowed.

"Hey! Where's your luggage, miss?"

"Uh—it's already been sent out here."

"Okay. Happy landings!"

Happy landings, indeed. A happy ending was what Cherry wished for, but judging by the milling crowd in the terminal, she was not even off to a good start.

For one thing she could not see Tom Reese any-where. Nor could she see any police officers. Or was she at the wrong end of this big place? Cherry felt terrified at being alone in her pursuit. But she was unable to hunt for Tom for fear of losing sight of the Ottos and Dance. To keep them in sight, with-out their seeing her, meant ducking and backtrack-ing—not easy to do in a crowd. At last they sat down on a bench near the BOAC desk—British Overseas Airlines.

Cherry found an unobtrusive place to stand, where a desk and wall formed a corner. From here she had a long view in all directions; of the three, of whichever way Tom came in, and of Idlewild Terminal itself.

This main waiting room, low-ceilinged, narrow, and very long, was more like a long corridor. Branching off this corridor was a labyrinth lined with ticket-and-information counters of various airlines, and gates and doorways, with shops and restaurants; it was crowded with travelers and porters and uniformed airlines personnel hurrying around piles of hand luggage. Loud-speakers announced constantly in several languages the planes' arrivals and departures; above this clatter of voices Cherry could hear, in gusts, the dull roar of the planes and the wind outside on the airfield.

"A regular maze of halls and doorways and gates," Cherry thought. "It would be easy to lose track of that threesome."

She glanced over at them from her corner. They were arguing among themselves. Oh, where was Tom? If he had started at the same time she had, why wasn't he here yet? Surely his telephone call to the police could not have taken more than five minutes. Unless the police did not believe his story—?

Cherry glanced toward Dance and the Ottos just in time to see Willard Dance walk over to the BOAC counter. He put a question, with his usual bland smile, to one of the airlines men and pointed to the wall clock. The clerk said something to him, then chalked up on the blackboard a slightly delayed take-off time for the plane to London. Dance nodded, satisfied, and went back and explained to the Ottos.

"*London,*" Cherry thought, appalled, "they're fleeing to London," when a shrill wail pierced all the other noises of the terminal. It seemed to come from the highway, and rapidly grew louder and shriller. A police siren! It must be Tom coming with the police, at last.

The approaching siren made the party of three restless. Otto picked up his suitcases. Dance looked furtively around in all directions, felt in his inside pocket, then as quickly composed himself. Only Mrs. Otto's face gave away their fear.

The siren screamed so loudly that it was earsplitting. People in the terminal stopped talking. With his foot Dance nudged his suitcase closer to him, smiling mechanically. Cherry, still unwilling to let them see her, kept watching in the directions from which Tom could come. The siren stopped, just outside. Dance jumped to his feet.

Here came Tom, rounding a corner! He strode

rapidly along with two men wearing business suits —plain-clothes men, Cherry realized.

"Otto and Dance—at the BOAC desk!" she called, stepping into view. "Tom! Over there!"

"All right, Cherry!" He saw her and kept moving.

"They're going to London—"

Tom hurried over to Dance, with Cherry right behind.

"Just a minute there, Dance!"

Dance and the Ottos took one look at the young people, seized their suitcases, and broke into a run. Down a smaller hallway they fled. The two plainclothes men ran to flank them. Immediately an incoming crowd surged in from the field, creating cover and confusion.

The police officers and Tom pushed through, but already the three were all but out of sight, darting and weaving through the crowd. Cherry, running as best she could, saw Dance veer off sharply to the alleyway on the right. Suddenly the crowd thinned as quickly as it had come, and Otto went plunging ahead over the low gate marked *Employees Only.* Right after him ran one plain-clothes man, and then Cherry realized that Mrs. Otto, unable to keep up with her husband, was puffing past her back into the main corridor.

"Stop that woman!" Cherry shouted and pointed.

"She's going into the flower shop! Stop her! The stout one!"

Guards ran into the florist shop. Cherry sped ahead. Out of the corner of her eye she saw Otto, awkward and encumbered by his luggage, stumbling just out of grasp of a plain-clothes man. He'd catch Otto in a matter of seconds, but Dance had vanished!

"Cherry!" Tom called. "Do you see Dance?"

"No— Yes!" she shouted back. "To the right!"

At the end of the passageway a ticket taker was picking himself up off the floor, with the help of passengers for the London plane.

"Out there!" he pointed to the dark field. "He brushed past me—"

Cherry and the two men ran to the edge of the field. It was dangerous out here, with giant propellers spinning in the dark and trucks speeding along. For a few moments they could not spot Dance anywhere. Then the landing lights of an incoming ship swept across the length of the field. In a glare brighter than daylight, Cherry saw Dance kneeling behind a pile of luggage.

"There—where the luggage is!"

Dance tried to run, but in an instant Tom forcibly stopped him. The plain-clothes man broke into their struggle. Dance subsided. They marched him back along the maze of corridors to the main room.

In front of the florist shop, Otto and his wife stood

at bay, trapped as much by the curious crowd as by the second policeman.

"All right, Mr. Reese," he said. "We have all the luggage, too. Let's go."

"Go? We'll miss our plane!" Dance said indignantly. "We're innocent, I tell you. You can't—"

Otto asked sullenly, "Where are we going?"

"To police headquarters for questioning." Tom could not keep the contempt out of his voice. "Mr. Briggs, will you need the young lady and myself?"

"Yes, come along. We'll want your testimony."

Otto, Mrs. Otto who was crimson with anger, and Dance were loaded into the police sedan with the two officers. Tom said he and Cherry would follow in a taxi.

"Listen," said Tom, just as their cab started down the highway. He had to shout above the roar; a plane climbed sharply and streaked away. "There goes the plane to London."

"Without them." Cherry had one glimpse of its lights.

It was a long, grim ride back to the city. Tom looked out the window, thinking, most of the way. Cherry did not feel much like talking either; she had to reflect on the testimony she would soon give. But it did help, in the midst of this terrible business, to have Tom hold tightly to her hand.

Christmas Eve

THE FIRST THING CHERRY DID ON ARRIVING AT police headquarters was to request permission to telephone Mrs. Julian's apartment. She explained that Mrs. Julian, too, had important testimony to give.

As she waited for the call to go through the police switchboard, Cherry glanced around the drab office. She was glad Tom was here; the police seemed remote; and the Ottos and Dance were coldly furious. The way they glared at her made her shiver. They were clever men; they might still walk out of here scot-free.

"Hello?" Mrs. Julian's voice came into the telephone. "Who is calling? . . . Why, Cherry! What a surprise. I came home late this afternoon—"

Cherry asked Mrs. Julian if she could come at once to police headquarters. Mrs. Julian promised to be there in a very few minutes.

Otto insolently took out a cigar and started to light it. When one of the plain-clothes men discouraged him, Otto protested, using the grand manner.

"Why, gentlemen, *why* am I and my party detained? Do you think it is amusing to manhandle reputable persons? Because a couple of young fools tell ridiculous stories!"

"No one manhandled you," the police captain barked at him. "You're here because serious charges, with partial proof, have been lodged against you."

"By those two youngsters?" Dance asked amiably. "Really, Captain! I can produce identification, references, bank letters, anything you wish." He reached into his pocket. "So can my friends, Mr. and Mrs. Otto. Ah—may I ask, can these two young adventurers do as well?"

He spread out his papers like a winning hand at cards. Captain Donnelly and his assistant did not want to see them.

"You expect us to believe you're innocent, when you led our men a chase out there at Idlewild?" Captain Donnelly turned his flinty eyes next on Cherry and Tom. "I expect you to back up your charges with proof. I'm going to question you, too."

Cherry did not know what charges Tom Reese had brought against the three. She could not very well ask him, or whisper to him, here. Probably he had brought charges in the name of the store. . . . Must tie in with what he'd discovered about Dance today. But what was that?

She hoped it was strong proof, because Dance could tell a smooth, plausible story and Otto had quite an authoritative manner. They might even cast doubts on Tom and herself before the questioning was over. What a way to spend Christmas Eve!

Then Mrs. Julian was admitted. She looked frightened and puzzled, but determined. Dance did not glance at her, and Otto and his wife loftily ignored her too.

"Come sit with us," Tom said in a low voice. He drew up a chair for Anna Julian beside Cherry. Cherry smiled encouragement, thinking what a lot had happened that Mrs. Julian did not know about. Not even about her music box.

There was no time to explain, though. The police captain was giving instructions to a male stenotypist and was ready to begin.

"I should like to request," Dance said in a silky tone, "that you discount the testimony of my employee, Mrs. Julian, since she is under suspicion of theft and she naturally—"

"That will do," said Captain Donnelly. He turned to a pale and stunned Mrs. Julian. "What can you tell us about Willard Dance and Elbert Otto? Take your time. Don't be nervous."

Mrs. Julian told of her acquaintance with the

two men, exactly as she had outlined it for Cherry.

"Then you never suspected either Dance or Otto," the police captain remarked. "And yet you worked closely with Dance?"

"Yes, I did, Captain. But when I made inquiries a few days ago in Boston at the headquarters of the art and antiques dealers' association, I was, to put it frankly, astonished at Mr. Dance's lack of—of professional standing. The bona fide men in the field had scarcely heard of him."

"And Otto?"

"They knew Mr. Otto, Captain, but they could not vouch for him."

"You report these men have little or no professional standing. Then what was the reason for Dance being in the antiques business? And Otto's business? And why the four thefts in quick succession?"

"*Four* thefts?" Mrs. Julian gasped. She turned to Cherry for confirmation. Cherry nodded, but waited her turn to speak.

The police began a systematic questioning of Elbert Otto and Willard Dance. At once both men insisted they had gone into their businesses legitimately, no matter in what light they appeared now. No, they were not in business together and never had been. Simply, they both were in the antiques business.

"We'll hear your story first, Mr. Otto," the police

captain ruled. "Remember that anything you say can be used against you in court proceedings. But I advise you to tell the truth."

Dance and Otto looked bored. The police captain leaned forward warningly. "We are in possession of certain highly interesting points about the Stoddard highboy, and we know a rose diamond necklace is in Dance's inside pocket." Dance nearly jumped out of his chair. "So you'd better tell the whole truth, both of you. The necklace, Mr. Dance! Or shall we search you?"

Dance handed it over in silence.

"Go ahead, Mr. Otto."

Otto turned ashen. When he spoke, his overbearing manner shrank to submissiveness.

Otto started his story with mention of his thorough education as an art expert and art historian. Equipped with this education, he had been employed for years by one or another of the large galleries as an assistant appraiser or an assistant consultant—modest routine staff jobs which brought him little or no reward or recognition. Otto wanted his own enterprise. He was growing older, his time to make a huge success was running out. Then the gallery which employed him went out of business and Otto was out of work. He decided to make the most of his unexpected freedom. A year or so ago he had rented a small gallery at 625 Madison Avenue and, with savings and with contacts, he went into business. Some of the art objects offered for sale were things which he and Mrs. Otto had bought up as bargains over a period of years, and enjoyed in their modest home. Others were art objects and antiques belonging to private owners who placed them with Otto on consignment.

At first Otto's business went well. He was convinced that a glittering future lay within his grasp. He was so hopeful that he rented Woodacres as a home for himself and his wife. Woodacres looked, and especially sounded, imposing, and it satisfied Otto's longings for grandeur. So Otto began to play the role which he had always envied.

But Otto was an art scholar, not a shrewd businessman, and he was not capable of running his own business. Against established galleries he could not compete; he remained obscure. He drifted into financial difficulties. Soon he was unable to pay the high rent at Madison Avenue. So Otto closed his commercial gallery, planning to use his home as his gallery.

"Otto Galleries? At Woodacres?" Mrs. Julian half turned to Cherry. Apparently, for all the woman's enthusiasm as a collector, she had never heard of Otto's being in business for himself. Mrs. Julian had known him only as an art consultant.

"Go on. What is your financial situation now?" the police captain questioned Otto.

"Well—I—" Otto nodded angrily at his wife, who was gesturing to him. "I think I should ask a lawyer, before I say anything more."

Captain Donnelly said, "This is not a trial, Mr. Otto. You aren't pleading anything here and we aren't passing judgment or sentence. Our job is to find out facts surrounding certain stolen art objects, and you're here to answer our questions. Mr. Otto, what is your present and recent financial situation?"

Otto answered reluctantly that during the period while his Madison Avenue gallery was rapidly failing, and then while he and his wife were readying a gallery at Woodacres, he did free-lance jobs as art consultant. One of his clients was Willard Dance.

Captain Donnelly made a note, but let that point go for the moment. "Were your fees as free-lance consultant enough to meet your expenses?"

"Please, they don't appreciate my husband!" Mrs. Otto burst out. "No, he did not earn much. Not enough. It has been hard. So then he tried to find another job, not just any job, of course. But I tell you, no one appreciates my husband!"

"So you didn't earn enough as a free-lance consultant, and you couldn't find the sort of position you wanted. I take it you refused to consider any other or lesser employment. How did you manage?" the police captain demanded.

"I—I owed several months' back rent for Woodacres," Otto admitted. "So I delayed paying my clients when I sold their goods," Otto muttered hastily. "And what's more, Dance owes me for my consultant services. Yes!"

"Don't blame it all on me!"

"Be quiet, Mr. Dance. You'll have your chance to speak. So, Mr. Otto, you misappropriated your clients' funds. You sold their goods and then pocketed all or part of what you received."

Otto did not deny the charge. Captain Donnelly asked if he wanted to say anything further. Otto merely stared at the floor.

"All right, Mr. Dance, we'll have your story, now."

"Well, as anyone can tell you, I was signally successful in the precious jewelry business," Willard Dance began. He was giving a good imitation of his usual easy assurance, Cherry thought. She was aware of Mrs. Julian listening with painful interest. "Fine jewelry both modern and antique is, as you know, sir, a related field to art objects and antiques."

Willard Dance had decided he could do even better in the antiques business. His late wife had been interested in antiques. Through her he had met Mr. Otto and Mrs. Julian's family who had collected antiques themselves. Also, he had inherited a few fine antiques from his wife.

Looking around for a location, Dance hit upon the idea of operating an antiques gallery within a fine, long-established department store. The store of his choice was Thomas and Parke; he applied there. Dance's earlier success in fine jewelry had impressed the department store, which investigated the business record of anyone applying for a concession and space within the store. Besides, the store liked his idea of an antiques department; it had never had such a department before. The store did not object to the fact that Dance was not experienced nor expert in antiques; the important fact was his proven business ability. Dance convinced the store that if he had an expert like Mrs. Julian and other qualified assistants, plus Mr. Otto's consultant services occasionally, he could repeat his earlier business success.

In addition, Willard Dance in his eagerness to become associated with this fine, prosperous store, offered a contract very favorable to Thomas and Parke. (Too favorable for his own business good, as it turned out.) Dance, confident, overoptimistic, had offered the usual ten per cent of his sales volume, plus an additional five per cent as inducement, guaranteeing the store a minimum of so many thousand dollars per year.

Space was assigned to him on the sixth floor. He engaged young Mrs. Anna Julian. Dance used his late wife's social standing and contacts to secure clients, and thus he obtained antiques on consignment. Willard Dance may have known little about antiques, but his genial, courteous, convincing manner persuaded people to let him put up their belongings for sale.

Dance paused. "I've done very well," he asserted, "at Thomas and Parke. *For* Thomas and Parke, too, I might add."

Tom Reese leaned forward. "May I mention something at this point, Captain? You wouldn't say, Mr. Dance, that you're by any chance in debt to the store?"

"Why—ah—as a store executive, Mr. Reese, you've surely seen the monthly statement for my department. You've seen for yourself that my department is doing well. Very well indeed." Dance ran his hand over his thinning hair. "I was perhaps overoptimistic about, possibly, the sales volume, but you'll concede—"

"I concede nothing. I've been checking up on you and your department all day today," Tom said bluntly. "Sure I've seen the statements, for months —*your* statements. You fixed them to look rosy, didn't you?"

Cherry was growing as excited as Mrs. Julian beside her. Dance indignantly started a denial, but Tom Reese drowned him out.

"Today, Mr. Dance, I checked up at the warehouse, and with the delivery service, and I pulled out the daily sales slips for your department for months back. Guess what I found, Dance? Your actual sales don't tally with those rosy monthly statements you turned in."

Tom's glance flickered in Cherry's direction, and she understood this was the discovery he had hinted at on the telephone. Otto was struggling to keep his face expressionless.

"I'll tell the police what happened, Dance, since you won't," Tom said.

Tom Reese discovered that Dance, like Mr. Otto, had drifted into financial difficulties—in Dance's case, because of overoptimism. Dance had guaranteed the store a minimum of so many thousand dollars—and then business in the antiques department just wasn't that good. He had been covering up that fact by systematically falsifying his records—claiming sales he never had made, for goods he never had to sell, claiming prominent customers who were out of the country. Thus from the store's viewpoint, Dance's department had appeared to be prospering and he had managed to conceal his debt.

"You owe Thomas and Parke, under the contract you were so eager for us to accept," Tom said dryly, "a sum well within six figures."

"As long as you know it, I won't try to deny it," Dance said. He had gone white but was still bland. "I suppose that's why I was notified I'm to be questioned on the day after Christmas?"

"Right," Tom said. "I suppose that's why you were too 'ill' to come into the store today—except after hours."

Dance smiled. The stenotypist was taking down the entire conversation.

"And I suppose that's why you were leaving for London tonight? You and your accomplices, the Ottos."

At the word *accomplices* Captain Donnelly again took charge of the questioning. Tom sat back in his chair, with a satisfied look at Cherry. But she was by no means satisfied yet.

The police captain did not waste any words. His questions were curt, penetrating. Otto and Dance, trapped now, supplied the facts.

Both men had found themselves in a tight financial spot. They discovered each other's predicament when Otto, needing money, pressed Dance to pay the consultant fees he owed. Dance had to admit he was unable to pay and pleaded for more time. Indeed, Dance did not plan to cheat either Otto or the store; he only hoped to stall for time.

But Otto could not and would not wait. He pressed Dance so hard that Dance told him of the fix he was in, and how he had falsified sales records. Once Otto learned this, he began to threaten exposure unless Dance "did something soon."

At first the two men had no plan, certainly no

plan for thefts. Then the Ming vase was stolen by a shoplifter. (The police were convinced of this, because a notorious shoplifter was known to have been passing through New York at that time.) But the store detectives, particularly Pierce, shunted suspicion onto Mrs. Julian. This happening suggested a way out to Otto—that he and Dance could steal antiques themselves out of Dance's department and use Mrs. Julian as a temporary scapegoat.

Dance disliked and was afraid of such a plan. He was upset when he applied for but was denied further insurance. He half agreed because Otto gave him no choice. Then he "got cold feet" and wanted to pull out. Otto hounded him—telephoned him repeatedly at the store, and visited him at the store, threatening to expose his false records.

"So that's why," Cherry thought, "he was so agitated about Otto's phone calls and visits!"

Dance got Otto to stop his telephone calls by falling in with the plan. He persuaded Otto to use discretion in sending messages. Phone or written messages were too risky, and the two men could not be seen together too often. To this end a marked newspaper, carried by Mrs. Otto, served as a means of communication between the two men for any urgent messages. The markings represented a simple code of prices, meeting places, persons, and dates; the messages surreptitiously dealt with their illicit plans.

Mrs. Otto transferred the newspaper to Dance on the busy main floor.

Mrs. Otto said proudly, "I also helped to find customers, and I helped my husband to receive them at Woodacres"—as if her wifely zeal placed her in a better light.

After the Ming vase incident provided them with a ready-made setup, Otto and Dance planned to steal the highboy and the rose diamond necklace. They would resell these abroad. Dance and the Ottos felt they would be fairly safe, because the insurance companies' detectives operated only within the United States. Otto and Dance had their plan figured carefully. Whatever money they could realize from the resale of the highboy and the necklace would tide them over until they established themselves in Europe.

They stole the highboy with the aid of a man, Eric Fox, who was Mrs. Otto's cousin. Fox was the one who posed as an "agent." He came to the department so that the sale would have all the aspects of a "straightforward" transaction. As Cherry already knew from Tom, the highboy was delivered to a nearly empty Fifth Avenue house. This address was rented for a brief period by Mr. Otto, under an alias. Immediately after the store delivered it, the cousin shipped the highboy out of the country to England. Speed was essential, before police and customs could be alerted. Eric Fox, the so-called agent who was wanted, then followed the highboy at once by air to London. Once there, he located a possible customer for it. At this distance the customer could not know that the famous highboy was stolen. Fox had also been making preparations for the arrival of his cousins and Dance.

As for the rose diamond necklace, Otto and Dance both realized that stealing insured goods which belonged to estates and individuals was a racket that could not last long, before the police and insurance companies became aware of it. They knew their time was running out; they knew they would have to flee abroad. Deliberately, because of the investigations, Dance left the taking of the diamond necklace to the very last moment. It was his department's most valuable object, the most easily transported and converted into cash. Dance and Otto needed money above and beyond their plane fares, to live on when they reached England, and until they could actually sell and get paid for the highboy.

"What's that?" the police captain asked sharply.

Otto was grumbling that he had warned Dance not to go back to the store for the necklace "—I never trusted that nosy nurse. Wasn't it bad enough that she traced the music box to Woodacres?"

"What!" Mrs. Julian exclaimed. "My music box? Did they steal that, too? Oh, Cherry—"

Cherry touched Anna Julian's arm and whispered, "Wait. Let's see what happens."

Captain Donnelly questioned the three culprits about the music box. Otto admitted it was a blunder to take the music box at such a touchy time, and particularly when Cherry was taking so much interest in Mrs. Julian's situation. But Otto had a quirk, a passion for music boxes, and he could not resist taking this one. He saw it and fell in love with it on the afternoon of the special exhibit. His using it as an illustration to his speech was a convenient way of getting it out of the showcase and into his hands. Then it took only a little dexterity to slip it into his capacious brief case. The crowd, and Otto's authoritative manner of handling art objects, covered him up nicely. True, store detectives were on duty at the special exhibit, but Otto gambled on their not keeping any particular watch on an established art expert. If anyone had challenged his taking the music box, Otto had planned to say he was going to show it at a customer's home.

Dance was obliged by now to back up Otto in whatever he did. After the exhibit, Otto simply took the music box back to Woodacres with him in the familiar bulky brief case which he always carried, and which therefore did not excite any suspicion. Dance waited several days to report the loss of the music box, thus allowing time to cover up Otto's taking it, and time in which to get Mrs. Julian out of town. For sooner or later she surely would have asked where her cherished music box was. With Mrs. Julian out of the way—and if only the nurse minded her own business!—they'd hoped to be far away before the investigators got on their trail. But after Cherry Ames had discovered the music box was at Woodacres, they knew they must clear out at once.

"To think I didn't even know it was stolen!" Mrs. Julian said.

"I'm glad you didn't know." Cherry smiled at her. "Besides, I think you're getting it back right now, as a kind of Christmas present."

During the recital of facts, one of the plain-clothes men, Briggs, went through the Ottos' and Dance's suitcases. From Otto's largest suitcase Briggs lifted out the familiar hand-painted music box.

"Is this it, Mrs. Julian?" the police captain asked.

"Oh, yes, yes, it is! I'm so happy and relieved to see it again, Captain."

"Well, Madam, you can thank this young nurse."

Mrs. Julian turned to Cherry. "Cherry—Captain Donnelly—what about the suspicions of me?"

"You are now absolved of any question of guilt," the police captain told her. He explained briefly. Of the four thefts, Otto and Dance had been responsible for three. Who took the Ming vase was still not finally established, but by process of elimination, the police believed the notorious shoplifter, in New York at that time, to be the thief. Two salespersons and a supervisor had recalled seeing the shoplifter in Thomas and Parke on that day. A Ming vase, answering the right description, had surreptitiously been offered to a gallery dealer in Boston only last week. The police were working on leads and expected to apprehend the shoplifter soon.

"As for ourselves—?" Dance said blandly.

"As for you gentlemen, and you, Mrs. Otto," said Captain Donnelly, "you are now under arrest!"

A police lieutenant opened the door and escorted them out. Over his shoulder Otto made one last gibe: "You will never trace Eric Fox or the highboy."

"Certainly we will. A teletype went out ten minutes ago to the British police and customs agents."

Captain Donnelly escorted Cherry, Tom, and Mrs. Julian to the door. He thanked all of them, and Cherry in particular, for their fine help.

The three of them rather dazedly went out into the quiet street. Church bells were ringing, and it was starting to snow.

"I had almost forgotten that it's Christmas Eve," Cherry said. "Merry Christmas, Tom! Merry Christmas, Mrs. Julian!"

"Cherry, you've given me a wonderful Christmas gift," said Mrs. Julian. "So have you, Tom Reese. I can't quite realize yet that I'm free of all suspicions!"

Tom smiled and smiled. "I'm not much good at making speeches, but I feel pretty happy myself. Mrs. Julian, how about coming to the party with us?"

"I've had enough excitement for one evening! If you'll just put me in a cab—"

Anna Julian kissed Cherry good-by. Cherry and Tom waved until the taxi turned the corner.

"I'm so glad for her," Cherry kept saying. "So glad. I can hardly wait to tell Gwen and Aunt Kathy —she's at No. 9 this evening, too—and all the crowd."

"Tell *me* something," Tom said.

"Anything!"

"Are you and I *ever* going to have our Christmas Eve date?"

"Right now, sir."

"Then hop in." Tom held open the door of another taxi. "It's about time! We're going to have a wonderful evening, or I'll know the reason why!"

Off they drove to No. 9.

Cherry felt very happy. This evening she'd enjoy the party and being with Tom. Early tomorrow she would fly home to Hilton, for gifts and a feast and a family visit.

"It's beginning to feel like Christmas Eve," Cherry told Tom. "You know, now that we have the mystery solved and out of the way, I can really say Merry Christmas!"